SANCHIA'S
SECRET

SANCHIA'S SECRET

BY

ROBYN DONALD

MILLS & BOON®

First published in Great Britain 2000
Large Print edition 2001
Harlequin Mills & Boon Limited,
Eton House, 18-24 Paradise Road,
Richmond, Surrey TW9 1SR

© Robyn Donald 2000

ISBN 0 263 16752 6

Set in Times Roman 16½ on 18 pt.
16-0301-51544

Printed and bound in Great Britain
by Antony Rowe Ltd, Chippenham, Wiltshire

CHAPTER ONE

'SHE won't sell? Why not?' Caid Hunter barked into the telephone. Eyes narrowing into intense slivers of blue, he propped a muscular thigh against his desk and stared unseeingly through the window at the twin towers that dominated the business district of Kuala Lumpur.

'I don't know. Her letter simply said Waiora Bay wasn't for sale.' His manager in New Zealand sounded startled—his boss didn't normally overreact to setbacks.

Summoning the cool intelligence that made him respected and feared throughout the Pacific Rim countries, Caid leashed his anger and leaned over to punch a couple of computer keys. His electronic diary opened out on the screen of the laptop. 'It's what—two months?—since her aunt died?'

'I went to Miss Tregear's funeral on the twenty-eighth of September, so it's just over two months.' The manager spoke crisply. 'Ms

Smith was quite adamant that Waiora Bay wasn't for sale. I can fax you her answer if you want to see it.'

A hot urgency stirred Caid's senses as he visualised Sanchia Smith—a stubborn chin, hair the colour of midnight shimmering over pale shoulders, and a body that had changed from lanky slenderness to elegant, innocent seduction between one Christmas and the next.

A girl who kissed like a sinful angel, then froze in his arms.

It took most of his will-power to thrust the memories into the past where they belonged. 'No, I'll deal with it when I get back.'

He put the receiver down and stood gazing out over the humid, congested city. Presumably Sanchia was hanging out for a better offer. Caid's smile hardened. When she discovered she couldn't screw him for one cent more than her inheritance was worth, would her greenstone eyes blaze, that passionate, sultry mouth tighten into anger?

Squinting against the ferocious January sun, Sanchia eased her foot onto the brake, skilfully negotiating potholes and drifts of gravel as she turned onto the Waiora Bay Road.

Half a kilometre later, on the boundary of the highway system and Caid Hunter's land, gravel and potholes gave way to well-kept tarseal. Everything on Caid's big cattle station breathed good husbandry backed by a vast amount of money.

Of course, the principal of a large, international corporation could afford to seal his farm roads!

Deliberately Sanchia persuaded her tense joints to relax. Since Great-Aunt Kate's funeral she'd made the four-hour drive from Auckland to Waiora Bay several times so the loneliness was nothing new, and the slow curl of apprehension that flooded her body with fight-or-flight hormones was completely familiar; she was always afraid that Caid Hunter would be there.

Which was mild paranoia; after the fiasco of three years before he'd probably made sure their paths hadn't crossed, and there was no reason to expect him to be in residence now.

And once she'd had this last holiday at the Bay, she'd never return.

Perhaps she should have followed her first instinct and come back for Christmas, toughed it out instead of giving in to friends who'd persuaded her to stay in Auckland for the festivities.

'Although I can *so* see why you want to go,' one had crooned, gazing sultry-eyed at the television screen as the credits rolled up on a documentary on high-flying businessmen. 'I'd be up there like a shot myself if I had a neighbour like Caid Hunter.' With a low growl she fanned herself vigorously with a newspaper. 'Talk about a splendid beast! When he smiled at the interviewer I swear her contact lenses fogged up. I bet he goes through women like a harvester at haymaking. Doesn't the camera love him? Is he really as sexy as that?'

Sanchia managed a laugh. It sounded a bit cracked, but neither of the other two women seemed to notice. 'Sexier.'

'I bet women fall at his feet in droves.'

'Oh, they do.'

Every summer girls had fluttered around Caid—glorious, self-assured creatures with pretty laughs and beautiful faces and bodies. Before she could stop herself Sanchia glanced surreptitiously down at the slight mounds beneath her thin shirt. How she'd envied those girls, their voluptuous, brazen breasts! And their confident sexuality.

Her flatmate sighed. 'Yeah, you could see the testosterone pounding through his veins. It's not fair that one man should have so much—an indecent amount of money, a face that's handsome enough to make your mouth water, and a brilliant business brain too!' She undulated sexily across the room, shaking her head so that her hair swung around her like a shampoo commercial. 'As well as being tough enough to grab a huge conglomerate like Hunter's by the neck when he wasn't much more than a kid, shake it out and strip it down into the leaner, more efficient, infinitely more profitable business that's taking on the world today. Where does this gorgeous man live? I might go looking for him.'

Rose, the owner of the house, laughed. 'Didn't they say he's based in Australia?'

Sanchia shrugged. 'He has houses all over the world.' Yes, she'd achieved the right casual, mildly amused tone.

'I could cope with a man who has houses
all over the world,' Jane decided generously.
'And because I'm always suspicious of pampered heirs, I thoroughly approve of the fact
that Caid Hunter had to fight to get his father's
company back on its feet. I do love a powerful,
masterful, dynamic man!'

'I don't think he was ever pampered,'
Sanchia told her, smiling with irony.

'He must have a thumping great character
flaw,' Jane said, frowning. 'There has to be a
catch. Does he cheat at Monopoly?'

'I've never played Monopoly with him.'
They'd played for much more dangerous
stakes. 'We said hello whenever we met on the
beach, and his mother used to ask us up to
dinner every holiday, but the Hunters were
well out of our league.'

Until the summer she'd finished university...

Rose asked, 'Is he likely to be at the Bay?'

Sanchia's stomach muscles knotted again.
'Possibly.'

'If he's not, will you mind being alone there
without a phone?'

'I won't be alone.' Two questioning glances persuaded her to expand, 'The farm manager and the caretaker both live nearby. For heaven's sake, both of you, I'll be fine—I want one last holiday there, that's all.'

Rose asked, 'A kind of pilgrimage?'

'Exactly,' Sanchia said gratefully. A pilgrimage to say a private, final farewell to Great-Aunt Kate, the only person who'd ever loved her unconditionally, and to the only place she'd ever called home.

And a pilgrimage that would achieve some sort of closure on the love affair she'd never really had.

So now her elderly car was leaving the smooth road across Caid's land to rattle down the hill through a remnant of coastal bush where tree-ferns cast starkly primeval shadows on the rutted track. Narrowing her eyes behind her sunglasses, Sanchia drove across the iron bars of the cattle-stop and over the grassy flat towards the small cottage.

On a short sigh of relief she braked and came to a stop. Small, rugged, wearing its eighty years with a jaunty, unashamed air, the cottage—never renovated and so called a bach—contrasted blatantly with the opulent mansion on the low headland to the west. To Sanchia's fury, her heart skipped a beat.

'You had a crush on him, but you grew out of it. It's dead, done and gone,' she pronounced firmly, dragging her gaze away from the trees that surrounded the Hunter mansion.

Her flatmates might admire a man who'd survived and won after being thrust into the cut-throat world of big business—but men like that were dangerous. And Caid Hunter wanted Waiora Bay. He had both power and the resources to fight her great-aunt's plans for it.

Trying to ignore the cold emptiness beneath her midriff, Sanchia switched off the engine and sat for a moment, letting her tired eyes feast on the scene before her.

Huge, crimson-tasselled pohutukawa trees sprawled between a newly mown lawn—for which she'd have to thank Will Spence, the Hunters' caretaker—and a glittering, sultry sea. Beneath the violent sun, sand blazed incandescently white. The tension behind her eyes began to wind more tightly as her gaze travelled to the leonine bulk of the island that sheltered the beach from northerly winds. A scattering of sails hinted at destinations beyond the horizon.

Tears aching in her throat, she pushed open the door of the car. Eventually she'd be able to remember the good times without grief, but she suspected it wasn't going to happen easily or quickly.

With an inelegant sniff, she manoeuvred her long legs out of the car and stood up.

Heat hit her like a blow, sucking the air from her lungs and pasting her thin cotton T-shirt to her back and breasts. After a swift tug at the clammy material, she accepted the sun's prodigal radiance on her shoulders and head, almost swaying with a poignant mixture of pain and mute relief.

With the soft hiss of the sluggish waves filling her ears, she bent to open the back door. As she touched the hot metal she yelped and leapt back, shaking her tingling hand.

'What the hell—?' A male voice, forceful and harsh and sexy.

Strong hands jerked her away from the car and Caid Hunter interposed his big, rangy body between her and the vehicle in a movement as unexpected as it was protective. 'What happened?' he demanded, lifting her hand and scrutinising it.

The foreboding that had lodged itself under Sanchia's ribs over the past weeks—ever since she'd received the offer for her great-aunt's property—expanded into an iceberg. Words clogging her tongue, she stared mindlessly up into eyes the intense blue of industrial strength cobalt.

Caid frowned. 'Did you burn yourself?'

She shook her head.

Handsome as the gods his mother's ancestors had summoned to rule the olive-silvered heights of Greece, Caid had inherited their fiercely compelling authority and self-assurance, their dark aura of power. During her adolescence she'd watched him with curious, fascinated eyes, secretly fantasising about him because he'd been unattainable and therefore safe.

Three years previously she'd crashed and burned against the difference between romantic fantasies and reality. Since then she hadn't seen him except in photographs and on television, usually with a glamorous woman clinging to his arm.

Although he still stole her breath away she lifted her chin and met his gaze squarely. Caid Hunter might have beauty and power, status and brains and money, but to her he was nothing more than an obstacle.

No, not *an* obstacle—*the* obstacle, the only person who stood between her and her great-aunt's dearest wish.

He persisted, 'If nothing happened why did you yelp?'

Forcing herself to sound briskly practical, she answered, 'I'm fine—you can let me go.'

Five foot ten tall herself, Sanchia didn't have to crane her neck to look into that spectacular face, although her eyes lifted six inches or so. Yet, broad-shouldered and narrow-hipped, with long, heavily-muscled legs, Caid swamped her. Already she could feel her stomach knotting, the stress from taut muscles.

Frowning, he dropped her hand and stepped back with a lithe grace that revealed effortless physical dominance. 'I've let you go,' he said laconically. 'You can relax.'

Across the short distance that separated them she saw his pulse beat strongly in the brown column of his throat, the slight sheen of moisture on his tanned skin.

Sanchia's heart gave a frantic shudder. In some distant region of her mind she thanked whoever had invented sunglasses for their minor protection. Her low-pitched voice sinking into huskiness, she explained, 'The car gave me a shock.'

He switched his gaze to the car. 'What's wrong with it?'

'Not it, me,' she said. 'Cars often shock me when I touch them after I get out. It's something to do with my body's electricity, I think.'

Oh, God! It sounded ominously close to a flirtatious come-on. She set her teeth in a smile that probably made her face look like a death-mask. 'I'm on a different wavelength from cars, and they let me know it.'

He was too sophisticated to openly eye her up and down, but the curve of his beautiful mouth—a trap for impressionable women—was tinged with satire. 'It must make life interesting.'

That smile smashed what was left of her composure with the energy of a well-aimed stone crashing through a bubble. 'Shocking,

actually,' she said, despising herself for her total lack of cool. 'I didn't expect to see you
here. How are you...' She hesitated a mini-
second before ending, '...now?'

'I'm fine, Sanchia.' A lazy mockery simmered just below the words. 'And you?' This
time the blue eyes skimmed her from head to
feet.

Although his glance didn't linger enough to
be impertinent or threatening, intent male interest smouldered like a shuttered flame behind
it.

Terrified and exhilarated, she wished she'd
worn jeans instead of exposing her long legs
in shorts. Using a deliberately formal tone to
distance herself, she said crisply, 'I'm very
well, thank you.'

'I was sorry to hear that your great-aunt had
died.'

The deep, almost harsh voice with its sensual undertone even sounded sorry. The
Hunters had been very kind; his mother had
sent flowers with a sympathetic note that had
made Sanchia cry, Caid had written a brief but
genuine letter of condolence, and a represen-

tative from the Auckland office of his firm had attended the funeral.

'It's the way she'd have chosen to go,' Sanchia returned gruffly.

'Dying peacefully in your sleep the night after your eightieth birthday party is the way we'd all choose to go,' Caid Hunter observed, 'but it's hard on the ones left behind.'

'I'm fine,' she said, as though saying it often enough could make it true.

'Grief takes time, but eventually it becomes bearable.' There was an odd pause, a kind of hesitation in the atmosphere, before he resumed blandly, 'So here you are, Sanchia, all grown up and more lovely than ever.'

And again he let his gaze wander, if such a leisurely survey could be likened to anything as indecisive as wandering. Heat and ice chased each other across her skin when his blue eyes narrowed and turned molten.

Apart from good skin and long legs, and her eyes, big and darkly green in their fringe of black lashes, Sanchia knew she had no claim to beauty, so the interest and speculation in his scrutiny were false. Although he couldn't guess at the darts of excitement arrowing through her, he understood the effect he had on the opposite sex. It was there in his stance—formidable, self-confident—in the smile that tucked up the corners of his mouth, in the amusement glinting in the dense blue depths of his eyes.

'So,' she said sweetly, 'have you. Grown up, I mean. And very nicely. Your mother must be proud of you.'

'Mothers are noted for their pride in their offspring.' The half-closed eyes darkened. 'What did I say?'

He saw far too much. Sanchia let her lashes droop and infused her voice with mock innocence. 'Simply that mothers are noted for pride in their children. I agree.'

His expression hardened. A glint in his eyes sent an unmistakable warning as he said silkily, 'Mockery gives your mouth an entirely too seductive pout, did you know? So why did you flinch? Wasn't your mother proud of you?'

In a reflex action as automatic as the emotion that caused it, Sanchia stiffened her spine. 'She died before I was interested in anything except her love.'

His mouth straightened but he left the subject, although she'd bet he'd filed her response somewhere in that formidable brain. Under 'To be Revisited' probably.

Glancing at the back seat of her car, piled high with three weeks' necessities, he asked smoothly, 'Can I help you carry that inside?'

A smile pasted onto her lips, Sanchia said, 'It's no use, Caid; I'm not going to sell Waiora Bay to you.'

There was a moment's silence. His thick black lashes focused the glance that cut through her defences like the blue blade of a sword, lethally probing. Any show of weakness might awaken an instinct for conquest. A chilly trickle of sweat inched down Sanchia's spine. Caid hadn't made a success of a huge international business without being a very keen predator indeed, and it was in the nature of the beast to hunt down anything that ran.

Crisply, her face still and proud, she added, 'Not now, not ever.'

'Why not?'

Sanchia bit off the words hesitating on the tip of her tongue. Summoning her flattest, most uncompromising tone, she said, 'Because it's not for sale.'

His cobalt eyes grew even keener. 'I've made you a fair offer. I don't plan to raise it.' His voice stood the hairs across the nape of her neck to attention.

'Whether you raise it or not is irrelevant,' she stated, snatching back her composure as it took to its heels. A heady sexual attraction warred with prudence; she ignored both to say recklessly, 'I hate the thought of the Bay being carved up so rich people can build ostentatious beach houses that are only used a couple of weeks each year.'

'My mother and I spend more than two weeks a year here.'

Heat stung her skin. 'I know. I didn't mean you—'

He interrupted, 'It doesn't matter. I don't intend to develop the Bay.'

'You won't develop it because I'm not selling it.'

'Are you planning to live here?' He flicked a razor-sharp glance at the cartons in the back of the car.

Gently, each word clear enough to shatter crystal, Sanchia said, 'I work in Auckland. I'm up here on holiday.'

'Sanchia, why don't we forget that three years ago I wanted to make love with you and you ran away as though you'd found yourself wanting to go to bed with a werewolf?' he said, his deep voice rasping across her nerves with shaming erotic effect. 'The letter you left made it quite clear that you didn't want to go down that road. It's over, and I don't bear you any ill will. Let's move on from there.' He held out a strong, long-fingered hand.

Even though Sanchia had always known she'd been merely a summer diversion, his acceptance of her abrupt decision to leave had shattered some vulnerable part of her. For a couple of months—oh, why not admit it? For at least a year!—she'd hoped that he might care enough to follow her. But he hadn't.

This, however, was different; this was business, and he wanted more than her untried body.

Great-Aunt Kate had always said that a gentleman waited until a woman indicated she wanted to shake hands. If the slow, heart-shaking smile Caid gave her was any indication, his mother had taught him the same thing, but his hand remained steadily out-thrust until Sanchia reluctantly put hers into it.

He didn't mash her bones together as some men did, and neither did his clasp linger, yet the touch of those lean, powerful fingers reached all the way to secret places inside her body, sent a mysterious knowledge shivering through her.

Damn, she thought frantically. Oh, *damn*! It was happening again, and even though she knew her response was a pathway to disillusionment, she couldn't control it.

When he released the swift, sure pressure, it felt like deliverance and abandonment at the same time.

Sanchia's weighted lashes lifted. He wasn't smiling; his blue gaze was fixed on her mouth. Beads of sweat sprang out at her temples, dampened her palms.

Lazily, almost noiselessly, he murmured, 'I have an odd desire to see my name on your lips, to hear your throaty, summery voice say it again.'

Caid wondered how she'd respond to the open provocation in his tone, his words, even as he wondered what the hell had got into him.

No, he knew what had got into him. From the moment he'd watched her long, long, superb legs unfold from the car he'd been ridden by a need so brutal he'd barely been able to control his own mind.

Not that his *mind* had much to do with this elemental aberration prowling his body with all the deadly determination of a tiger on the hunt. Why didn't she take off her sunglasses? By hiding those exotic green eyes, the dark lenses concentrated his attention on her luscious mouth.

What would it taste like now? What would *she* taste like? Incredulously he realised that his skin was tightening in a primitive warning, his muscles flexing in readiness. Fighting to subdue the hunger that threatened to drown his intelligence in a flood of lust, he waited for her reply.

It came with an infuriating dignity that should have quenched the heat gathering in his groin. With a return of the baffled frustration only she aroused, he remembered anew the way she'd taken refuge behind a distant, self-contained remoteness.

'Caid,' she said coolly. 'Satisfied?'

'No, but I'll settle for your signature on an option form,' he said, watching her intently.

That enticing mouth compressed as she hesitated.

Cynically aware that he'd left himself open to an attempt at extortion, he waited. It would be interesting to see what she'd do if he offered her a good lump sum of money right now.

His eyes skimmed her clothes, read *chainstore*. Such an exquisite body should be draped in silk. And there had to be something wrong with that elderly car. Was she a woman to be seduced by instant money?

No; if she was, she'd have slept with him three years previously.

Even as he wondered about the rush of altruism to his brain, he drawled, 'I would, of course, pay for that assurance.'

She paused, her square chin lifting a fraction. 'What's the going rate for an option?'

A dollar.

Negligently, his tone casual and off-hand, he mentioned a sum of money—enough, he guessed, to give her a considerable jolt.

She took her time to answer, turning her head to survey the beach. A neat profile, but not exactly beautiful, not even pretty, although her features were fine and regular. Caid had always liked cool, restrained women, but what stirred his hormones when he looked at Sanchia Smith was the repressed passion he knew existed beneath that reserve.

With her black hair shimmering around her shoulders, pale, translucent skin and a mouth that had summoned forbidden fantasies, she'd always looked fey, enchanted—like a perilously exotic woman from the ancient fairy stories. Now, in old shorts, and a damp T-shirt moulded to small, high, tantalising breasts, that potent, sensuous bloom had turned into something that caught his breath.

Caid found himself wondering if she was still a virgin. It didn't seem likely, and why should he care? He'd never demanded virginity from his lovers.

God, what the hell was he thinking? This was business, not sex! Get your mind, he commanded grimly, above your belt.

It was impossible to tell what was going on inside her head until in a crisp, no-nonsense voice, she said, 'That's a lot of money for nothing.'

Something in her tone, in her square shoulders and tilted chin, reminded Caid of the teenager who'd looked past him and through him, over him and around him—anywhere but at him. Need burning in his gut, he heard her say, 'I'll sign an option if it will make you happy, but I'm still not selling.'

An X-rated fantasy of her making him happy, in full colour and with sound and kinaesthetic effects, blocked Caid's thought processes. Angry at the effort it took to reimpose control, he said curtly, 'Think it over before you make a decision.'

'I don't need to think anything over because I've already made the decision.'

At last she turned towards him, face shuttered against him as she waited for him to go. For a split second he toyed with the idea of helping her unpack, but much more of this and his clamouring body would betray him.

'I'll bring the papers down this evening,' he said.

No doubt, Sanchia thought, you didn't get to be a big-time tycoon unless you were prepared for everything. 'You travel with option forms?' she asked ironically. 'It's the holidays, if you remember, and every solicitor in New Zealand is at the beach until at least halfway through January.'

'I always have options,' he said. Some underlying note in his voice caught her attention as he finished crisply, 'So I'll see you tonight.'

CHAPTER TWO

SANCHIA stood motionless until Caid's imperious presence had disappeared into the green gloom of the pohutukawa trees. Expelling her breath with a whoosh that spun her brain, she muttered, 'Oh, hell!'

It had been too much to hope fate would make sure their visits to the Bay didn't coincide.

With jerky, abrupt movements she bent to haul the nearest carton out of the car, fighting a powerful, irresistible tug at her senses. One look at Caid and it had all come pouring back—the heady, dangerous compound of desire and longing and abject, hidden terror.

As she walked across the grass to the bach and dumped the groceries down on the lid of the gumboot box she thought stoutly that she was better able to deal with it now than three years ago.

She unlocked the door, stepping back as a wave of hot, stale air fell out of the building.

Did he still want her? Her mouth twisted sardonically. Why should he, when he could have his pick of the most beautiful, sophisticated, suitable women in the world? He'd certainly taken his time about looking her over, but that meant nothing.

Was he paying me back? she wondered, picking up the carton. I don't suppose many women have said no to Caid Hunter. Perhaps he was trying for a little revenge?

After setting the box onto the kitchen bench she opened up the bach, turning on the power, switching on the gas so that she'd have hot water, fiercely quelling a fresh surge of grief when she pushed back the bifold doors. A fresh, salt-scented breeze curled up from the beach, brushing away the mustiness.

Her breasts lifted as she breathed in and out several times; she stared straight ahead, but after a few moments realised that her gaze had wandered stealthily to the roof of the Hunter house above its sheltering trees. If she craned her neck she could see the edge of the wide terrace overlooking the sea.

Nothing had changed; she still responded to Caid's powerful physical presence with all the poise and control of a kid in an ice cream shop. 'So why stand here mooning over him?' she asked the unresponsive air before stalking inside.

When the car had been emptied and her bed made up, when she'd revived the bach again with the small domestic sound of the refrigerator, when the last trace of dust had been scoured away and she'd showered herself clean of sweat and grime, she drank two glasses of water and made a salad sandwich, following its green and gold crispness with coffee.

Only then did she feel able to walk out onto the wide wooden deck, cross the lawn and stop in the dense shade of the pohutukawa trees.

Because a late, cool spring had delayed their flowering, crimson bunches of silk floss still burst from furry, silver buds to smother the leathery leaves.

Caid had kissed her for the first time under this one.

Pain twisted inside her. Leaning her hot forehead against the rough bark, she imagined that she could feel an old, old life-force slowly, inexorably, sweeping through the wood. How many times had she seen her great-aunt stand like that, drawing strength from a tree?

There was no comfort for Sanchia; nevertheless she faced the future with a bleak, driven determination. Great-Aunt Kate had trusted her to carry out a mission.

A heat haze shimmered over the sand, the dancing air lending an oddly eerie atmosphere to the classic New Zealand holiday scene— white beach, a cobalt sea intensifying to brilliant kingfisher-blue on the horizon, and a summer coast of bays and headlands, cliffs and harbours, swathed in carmine and scarlet and crimson.

Setting her jaw, Sanchia turned and walked across the springy grass towards the steep hill behind the bay, following a hint of a path beneath the trees. To the fading sound of the waves, she stepped lightly, cautiously, like an intruder.

Another ancient pohutukawa hugged a grassy knoll on the boundary between her aunt's land and the Hunter property, and each winter thousands of monarch butterflies found their way back to the tree to doze in the Northland sun along its sheltering branches, drinking from the tiny stream in the gully. Drowsy, almost immobile, they dreamed the winter away.

A few were still there, gorgeous, graceful things in their livery of orange and black. She stood for long moments watching, remembering.

The year she'd turned sixteen she'd noticed the pitiable flapping of a butterfly drowning in the creek. Still unsure of her suddenly longer legs, she'd raced down the hill to its rescue, landed awkwardly on a stone and wrenched her ankle.

Caid had found her sitting on the bank with the butterfly drying on her finger. Carefully, gently, he'd coaxed the bold orange and black insect from her hand to his, and transported it to a branch. Once he was sure it was going to be all right, he'd ignored her protests, scooped her up and carried her back to the bach.

She couldn't recall breathing or talking until he'd deposited her in a deckchair. Now she wondered whether it had been his complete lack of reaction to her, his lazy amusement and casual friendliness that had persuaded her to trust him five years later.

Or perhaps it had been the feel of his arms, the steady, amazing strength that had seemed so effortless...

'Interesting how much more wary these butterflies are than the ones that over-winter,' a voice drawled from the other side of the fence.

Flinching, Sanchia whirled to face Caid. 'Next time make a noise,' she retorted curtly, then bit her tongue, aware of her rudeness—and the susceptibility it didn't hide.

His black brows lifted. 'Certainly,' he said, a note of mockery underlining his words. Casual shorts and a T-shirt as black as his hair failed to strip him of that cool, powerful authority.

Glad she'd replaced her sunglasses, she muttered, 'I'm sorry, but you gave me a start. It's uncanny the way you sneak around.'

'Sneak?' His sculpted mouth twisted in irony. 'I resent that. If my presence disturbs you so much I'll whistle whenever I think you might be in the vicinity. You don't want to hear me sing.'

'Why not?' He had a marvellous speaking voice, deep and exciting, a voice that reached right inside and...

Sanchia stifled that train of thought.

'I can't carry a tune,' he told her cheerfully.

'Oh.' Her doubtful glance caught his smile. Because it stirred up emotions she'd tried very hard to forget, she said hastily, 'I wonder why these butterflies stay here?'

'They're foolish and frivolous. Any prudent, far-sighted monarch is in a garden somewhere, mating, and laying eggs to continue the species; these ones are wasting the summer heat.'

There was no suggestiveness in his words, yet her spine tingled.

'Perhaps they sense there's still time,' she parried. Disturbed by his narrow-eyed focus on the hair around her shoulders, she pushed the dark cloud back, holding it behind her head with one hand.

Caid said, 'A wise butterfly takes its chances quickly. You never know when a cyclone might hurtle down from the tropics.' He spoke lightly, as though the words meant nothing, but his glance settled on her mouth.

Sanchia felt the resonance of a hidden meaning. A forbidden sensation exploded in the pit of her stomach. Taking three quick steps into the sombre shade of the tree, she said, 'Cyclones are very occasional events here. The butterflies have plenty of time to enjoy themselves and still fulfil their evolutionary duty. Besides, it might be a ploy on nature's part to fill a gap. If they do their egg-laying late in the season the eggs mightn't be eaten by wasps.'

'There are always predators.'

Sanchia's skin contracted as though some of the chilling certainty in his tone had been translated into physical existence. They seemed to be conducting another conversation beneath the words, one depending on feelings and a ferocious physical awareness for its subtext.

Lightly she said, 'So your advice to the young butterfly is to grab every chance? Could be dangerous.'

'Life's dangerous. And butterflies could die at any time.'

Sanchia bit her lip, heard a soft oath and the sudden creak of the boundary fence as Caid swung over it. 'I'm sorry,' he said abruptly, his hand coming to rest on her shoulder. 'That was clumsy and obtuse of me.'

His touch exploded through her like wild-fire, dangerous, beautiful, filled with a hazard-ous lure.

'It's all right,' she mumbled. 'It wasn't you—or what you said. It just comes over in waves.'

'I know.' Strange that the textures of warmth and harshness were mingled in his voice. He lifted a hand to trace the trickle of a tear just below her sunglasses.

Sanchia's jerk was instinctive but the imprint of his long, lean fingers, tanned and graceful, burned into her skin as his hand fell to his side. She looked up and saw his beautiful mouth harden as he stepped back, giving her space to breathe.

'Great-Aunt Kate used to love summer,' she said, knowing it sounded like a peace offering.

He nodded. 'I remember her swimming every day, and striding along the beach in the morning looking like some ancient, vital nature spirit. She had such guts, such zest.'

'She didn't take any nonsense,' Sanchia said, her heart clenching, 'and she was brusque and sensible and plain-spoken, but she was infinitely kind.'

'You've never told me how you came to live with her,' he said neutrally.

'It's a long story.'

'And one you don't want to talk about.' Gleaming blue eyes examined her from beneath thick, straight black lashes.

His words challenged her into revealing more than she intended. 'My parents died when I was twelve and I had to live with my mother's sister. She was younger than my mother, and she didn't like spoilt kids—' and oh, was that ever an understatement! '—so after—after a while I ran away. Great-Aunt Kate found me and brought me here, and we worked out a system of living together.'

It had taken a lot of patience and love from a woman already elderly, a lot of effort on both their parts, and almost a year for Sanchia to learn to trust again.

'I remember when she brought you here,' Caid said unexpectedly. 'You were a tall, skinny kid, all arms and legs with hair that floated like spun silk behind you when you ran. That first summer I don't think I heard you speak, let alone laugh. My mother worried about you.'

Startled, Sanchia said, 'Did she? That was kind of her.'

'Mmm. She's a very kind woman.' He ran a forefinger down Sanchia's arm. Fire followed the light, swift touch.

He knew it too. In a voice that hovered on the border of amusement, he said, 'You're hot. I'll walk you home.'

She didn't want him back at the bach; struck by inspiration, she countered, 'Why don't we go via your place and I'll sign that option? Then you won't have to bring it down tonight.'

His mouth curved. 'Why not? Can I help you over the fence?'

She flashed him a look. 'No, thanks. I haven't forgotten how to climb a fence.'

Although under his eye she fumbled it, landing too heavily on the other side.

'My mother worried about you,' Caid explained, swinging over with a sure male grace, 'because she has a strong maternal streak. It's wasted with only me to lavish it on—she should have had ten kids. You reassured her the following summer when you'd grown a few inches, and we heard you laughing and saw that you were very fond of your great-aunt.'

'I didn't think you noticed us much,' Sanchia said, starting jerkily down the mown track.

Black brows shot up. 'I noticed you.' Watchful eyes beneath lowered lashes should have given him a sleepy air. They did nothing of the sort; the half-closed lids intensified both the colour and the speculation in his gaze.

Sanchia lifted her brows in return. With a composed, polite smile she replied, 'You were busy with your friends, and we hardly ever saw you except when you were sailing or water-skiing or windsurfing, or having a party on the beach.'

She'd seen him enough to fuel some heated fantasies, however! Innocent daydreams—a kid's crush without the heavy, hard beat of dangerous sexuality that pulsed through her now. That had come later.

The path dived in under the trees, releasing them into welcome shade. Apart from an early cicada strumming his strident little guitar, the foliage muffled and deadened sounds, cocooning them in a heavy, pressing silence.

Caid's lashes drooped even further. His mouth, an intoxicating combination of power and classical lines, curved. 'So you ignored us. How unflattering—especially as I was very aware of you,' he said softly. 'The first thing I used to do each summer was to impress on my friends that you were absolutely, totally out of bounds, and that if anybody made even a token gesture towards you I'd personally dismember him.'

Sanchia's mouth dropped open; his tone rearranged the cells in her spine, turning them into jelly.

'How kind,' she said, resisting the desire to lick suddenly dry lips. Humiliatingly, the thought of Caid warning off his friends appalled her yet sent shivery, sneaky frissons of excitement through her.

Rallying, she went on, 'The best sort of big brother—an unknown one.'

'Yes,' Caid said easily. 'It wasn't so bad until you turned sixteen and developed a figure like a supermodel—the year you hurt your ankle rescuing a butterfly, if you remember. Then I had to get very heavy. So did my mother.'

'I'm so grateful,' Sanchia said, striving for a brisk, matter-of-fact tone. Unfortunately she couldn't stop herself from continuing with the faintest snap, 'It sounds as though you kept a close eye on me.'

From the corners of her eyes she caught the flash of white teeth in a satirical smile. Infuriated, she stared stonily ahead.

'Only at the beginning of each summer,' he said, and added outrageously, 'To check up on progress, you understand.'

Sanchia snorted.

With infuriating amusement he went on, 'And then, three years ago, when you came back after university, I discovered you'd more than fulfilled all that coltish promise.'

He was using his voice as an instrument of seduction; its deep timbre and intriguing hint of an accent stroked along her nerves with the sensuous nap of velvet, at once caressing and stimulating.

How many women had lost their heads when he spoke to them like that? Dozens!

'I—remember,' she said foolishly, unnerved enough to miss seeing a large spider-web hanging from a manuka branch until it clung to her face, its panicked occupant racing towards the branch in a tangle of black legs.

Sanchia hurled herself sideways, her foot twisting over a root as she cannoned into the man beside her. 'Sorry!' she gasped, clutching instinctively at solid muscle.

Caid moved with lethal speed, his strong hands clamping onto her arms, wrenching her away from him as he hauled her upright. When he saw she wasn't going to fall, he wiped the remnants of the web from her cheek with a sure, gentle touch.

Her breath turned into lead in her chest; her gaze clung to the prominent framework of his face, the potent mouth. Although her hands were empty she could still feel his hot, fine-grained skin searing her palms.

'Is the spider all right?' she asked breathlessly.

His hand stilled; she looked up to meet incredulous eyes. Some small part of her brain realised dimly that they were standing a few centimetres apart, his blue gaze fencing with hers through the protective mask of her sunglasses. Pinned by those molten eyes, by his grip, she couldn't breathe, couldn't think, and her body sang an irrational song of feverish, primal need.

'The spider?' he asked harshly.

When she nodded he gave a hard, humour-less laugh. 'Why don't you look for yourself?'

Sanchia froze as he whipped off her sun-glasses, stepped back and released her, his face impassive.

She forced her glance past him and said, 'Oh, the spider's fine. P-probably cursing clumsy p-passers-by.'

With any luck Caid would think it was the close encounter with the spider that pitched her voice too high and caused that betraying hes-itation.

'Are you all right?' he asked curtly.

She made herself breathe. 'Yes. Sorry. I hate spider-webs on my face.' It was all she could trust herself to say because her voice sounded as though it was going to descend into an in-coherent, humiliating babble.

'You've experienced them often?'

'When I ran away in Auckland, before Great-Aunt Kate found me, I slept in a park and one morning I woke with a web over my face.' She shuddered. 'I'd dreamed I was dead, and for some reason the web convinced me that it had really happened.'

He took his time about scanning her face. Dazed, she thought she could feel his survey like a laser across her skin.

'That must have been an appalling experience,' he said evenly, and smoothed the sweep of one cheekbone with a tantalising thumb.

Fire and ice combined in that touch—at once smooth and abrasive, light yet sinking down into the very centre of her bones.

Summoning every ounce of will, Sanchia stepped back and muttered, 'As you saw, I still get a bit spooked by them,' and turned to blunder down the path.

From behind he asked, 'Don't you want your sunglasses?'

'Oh.' She stopped and held out her hand. 'Thank you.'

His smile as he handed them over told her that he expected her to stuff them back on. It was exactly what she wanted to do, hide behind them. Why on earth had she blurted out that grisly little experience in the park?

Gritting her teeth, she clutched the sunglasses in hand as she set off again. She was going to have to watch her disconcerting tendency to confide in him.

Caid rejoined her silently, a little too closely because the path was narrow. His bare arm brushed hers, and a bolt of electricity sizzled through her.

'What have you been doing these past few years?' he asked. He spoke in a calm, unhurried voice, as though nothing had happened.

Because nothing had. 'I've got a job at one of the technical colleges in Auckland—in a faculty office.'

He frowned. 'Why didn't you use your degree? I know you didn't want to teach, but people with Asian languages are in high demand all around the Pacific Rim.'

He'd taken two degrees at the same time, a high-powered commerce one and law. Sanchia shrugged. 'I discovered I had nothing much to offer an employer so I took a computer skills course and was lucky enough to find a clerk's job.'

'And is that what you are now?'

'No,' she said calmly. 'I've advanced a couple of steps.' And planned on advancing a lot more.

His keen look indicated that he'd picked up the ambition that fired her. 'Are you enjoying it?'

'Very much. Students from all over Asia study there so I'm picking up a good grounding in several other languages. And as I get free tuition I'm working my way through management qualifications.'

The path led to a small gate behind the Hunter house. The thinning trees allowed light to blaze down in golden medallions through the leaves. Caid reached past her and opened the gate, standing back to let her go through first.

Relieved, Sanchia donned her sunglasses as they walked out into the sun's full power and crossed the closely mown lawn. It looked, she thought, trying hard to be dispassionate, like a picture in an expensive magazine. Shaved green lawn, gardens in full summer array, the house shaded by pergolas, and on two sides the glamour of the sea.

And the man beside her, as handsome as any model she'd ever seen in a magazine and infinitely more formidable. She said clumsily, 'I should have worn a hat.'

'You should. That milky skin must burn like tinder.' Intolerable as the heat from a furnace, his glance touched her bare arms, her face.

'Everybody burns in this sun,' she returned swiftly.

Although he probably didn't—he had his mother's built-in golden tan along with her black, black hair. Sometimes when he spoke Sanchia could hear Mrs Hunter in a certain intonation, an un-English arrangement of words.

Quickly, before he could give her another of those intimidating looks, Sanchia added, 'I slather myself with sunscreen every time I go out.'

'Good. Skin like yours should be cherished.' Again that cynical, caressing note in his voice mocked the compliment.

Irritated by her heated, mindless response, she said shortly, 'All skin should be cherished.'

'No doubt, but yours is a work of art.'

'Thank you,' Sanchia replied tautly.

Did he hope that a meaningless flirtation would persuade her to sell Waiora Bay? No, that instant physical response was real enough, and she wasn't the only one feeling it.

But he could well intend to use it as a weapon.

Side by side they walked into the welcome coolness of a creeper-shaded terrace. Sanchia's sandals clicked on the ceramic tiles as she followed him between loungers and chairs towards a wall of pushed-back glass doors.

'Come in,' Caid told her, standing back so she could go before him into the big sitting room beyond.

Sanchia had never forgotten the atmosphere of casual elegance, of European glamour and comfort that permeated Caid's house. Reluctantly, feeling she was yielding an advantage, she removed the sunglasses and, without giving herself time to harness the clutch of bumblebees in her stomach, said, 'I'm not open to persuasion on the future of the Bay.' Fixing her gaze on a blur of flowers in a magnificent vase, she underlined her statement as delicately as she could. 'It will probably save a lot of time and useless manoeuvring if I tell you that you won't coax Great-Aunt Kate's estate from me.'

He said in a voice so cold it froze her every cell, 'I don't do business that way, Sanchia.'

'I wasn't meaning—'

'Then what were you meaning?'

Sanchia faced him, her chin angling up as she grabbed for her scattered wits. 'I'm not going to be won over by an appeal to greed, either. Why offer me a couple of thousand for an option to buy the Bay when I'd made it obvious I didn't want to sell? You know perfectly well that an option is usually sealed by a coin.'

For a racing moment she thought she saw a hint of respect in the vivid eyes.

'There's no set legal fee,' he said drily. 'An option to buy is a business decision, and the amount offered to cover it is decided on by the two people concerned.'

'But it's usually no more than a token—a dollar. You were testing me.' She held his gaze a second longer. 'You can pay me a dollar for the option, but I'm not going to change my mind about selling.' And because his smile flicked her on the raw, she finished with a foolish bravado, 'However much you try to intimidate me, or however charmingly you flirt with me.'

His smile vanished, but before she had time to exult he advanced on her, his silent grace a threat. Although Sanchia's stomach lurched, she refused to back away.

'This,' he said, resting his thumb on the jumping pulse in her throat, 'has nothing to do with the document *you* made the decision to sign.'

Gently, without pressure, his hand curved around her throat, the fingertips moving slightly against the sensitive nape of her neck, producing a tiny friction as purposeful as it was erotic. 'Neither has the fact that your eyes are a smokier, more sultry green than I remember, and that your mouth is a miracle...'

Sanchia looked up into metallic eyes and saw the effort he had to put into relaxing his fingers. Inside her a latent hunger uncoiled, began to move through her veins like the tide of life greeting an arctic spring, long-awaited, unrestrainable.

'Nothing to do with business at all,' Caid repeated dispassionately, his voice deep and hard. 'I find you very attractive, very appealing—I have ever since you turned sixteen. But I do not intimidate women, nor force them into my bed, and I don't use lies to seduce them into making decisions either. Am I forcing you now?'

'No.' The word splintered with repressed emotion—*terrifying* emotion—a passionate, wild desire that warned of sensual meltdown.

Slowly, whispering across the surface, his fingertips tantalised her skin as his thumb noted the increased thudding of her pulse. Sanchia shivered.

Bending his head, he said fiercely, 'You can walk away if you want to.'

She lifted heavy eyelids. 'I don't want to.'

Triumph flashed in the blue eyes. 'Good,' he said, and kissed her.

It was like an earthquake: the foundations of her world shifted and she no longer had any reference points for normality as sensation stormed through her. Shattered by the violence of her response to Caid's seeking, demanding mouth, Sanchia gave up trying to think and surrendered to the astonishing pleasure his kiss summoned.

Some time later she surfaced; locked in his arms, she was pressed against him from shoulder to thigh so that his arousal was more than obvious.

Appalled, she tried to pull away, but he lifted his head and said harshly, 'It's too late for that.'

'Oh, no, it's not,' she muttered, beating back the first icy trickle of fear. 'I must be mad. Caid, let me go!'

'So nothing has changed,' he said coldly, releasing her immediately. 'Kissing is all right but I must go no further. Why, Sanchia?'

Twisting away, Sanchia ran a shaking hand through her hair and whispered, 'I won't let this happen again!'

He showed his teeth. 'Hell, isn't it?' he agreed sardonically. 'Just one of those mad attractions that shatter kingdoms and ruin lives.' His eyes glinted. 'Perhaps you have such a powerful effect on me because I spent several summers watching you grow up. And one infinitely frustrating holiday trying to get past the iron-clad barriers that slammed in my face whenever I touched you. What's your excuse?'

Weighed down by reaction to the adrenalin overdose, Sanchia blinked and gathered the tattered remnants of her wits about her. 'Look, produce this piece of paper, I'll sign it and say goodbye, and we can forget that the—that this ever happened.'

'Coward,' he taunted.

'Absolutely,' she agreed fervently, thrumming with thwarted desire now that he'd let her go. 'I like a peaceful life and you're very definitely not peaceful. We've got nothing in common.' She dragged her gaze from his enigmatic face to stare around the room. 'Where is this option?'

'In the office.' But even as he nodded towards a door he said caustically, 'We have one thing in common, Sanchia—a consuming physical passion that's going to drive both of us crazy unless we do something about it. Why does it scare you so much? I won't hurt you.'

Sanchia swallowed to ease her arid throat. For a second panic clutched her, and with it a soul-destroying shame. Had he guessed? No, she decided with a swift spurt of relief, not yet. She strode across the room in front of him, flinging over her shoulder, 'I don't want an affair with you!'

'So you said three years ago. Why, Sanchia? Does passion terrify you so much?'

If only he knew...

She said jerkily, 'I'm not cut out for being a diversion, a pretty toy to be used and then discarded. You forget that while you were checking the length of my legs and whether I laughed or not, I was watching girls chase you. You didn't run very far, they didn't last very long—just long enough to break their hearts. I noticed the pattern early and it's not one that fits me. I need independence—to lead my own life, for myself.'

'And does your wonderful independence,' he queried in a dangerously silky voice, 'keep you sated and warm at night?'

'There are more important things in life than sex.'

He said something swift and angry in Greek, the language she had stubbornly refused to even consider learning. Switching to English, he said, 'Or perhaps you work off that violent physical appetite of yours with strangers, with casual affairs?'

She'd kept so much from him she was tempted to add a whopping lie, but she said stiffly, 'I don't approve of petty, sordid affairs.'

So unnerved that she barely understood her own words, she yanked the door open and walked through, frowning when she saw she was in a passage. 'Which way?'

'To the left, second door down.'

He walked beside her, close enough to intimidate, not close enough to touch. Just as well—she'd go up like a fireball if he laid so much as a finger on her. All right, so it was merely the physical passion he'd called it, but oh, God, it was overwhelming—like being branded by him so that her body registered him, recognised him, yearned to know him intimately.

Feared him.

Because the one time she'd tried to break past the arbitrary limits her body had set, it had frozen in fierce, unreasoning rejection.

He asked coolly, 'Does that mean there have been no affairs—or just no petty, sordid ones?'

'Mind your own business!' she retorted fiercely.

'You are the person who used the word *sordid*.' Stone-faced, he pushed the door open and stood back to let her through. 'And any affair between us would never be petty. I promise you that.'

CHAPTER THREE

THAT last comment didn't just *sound* like a threat, Sanchia realised with an inner shiver as she glanced at Caid's harshly beautiful face, it definitely *was* one.

The intriguing scent—faint, potent—of aroused male made her grit her teeth as she walked past him into a room set up as an office. Apprehension roiled her stomach as she stopped in the middle of the room and waited in silence while he bent to open the door of a safe.

She'd hoped counselling would free her of the suffocating fear of sexuality that had preyed on her for so long, but, in spite of the therapist's insights, ugly terror still lurked behind the fireflash of desire.

Caid straightened and put a piece of paper on the desk. 'You'd better read it first.'

'I don't sign anything without reading it,' she said huskily, but she had to concentrate ferociously on the print dancing in front of her eyes.

It was quite straightforward. When she came to sell the land known as such and such on the district plan she would offer it to him first, the price to be negotiated then. If he refused it she was at liberty to do what she wanted with it.

Sanchia read it through twice before handing it back. 'It seems fair enough.'

'Did you know that all the land in this area has just been revalued?'

She gave a brief nod.

'Waiora Bay's blue water title adds quite considerably to the value of the place because it means no one can land on the beach.' Caid paused, and added smoothly, 'I believe the rate increase this year is somewhere in the vicinity of twenty-five per cent.'

Sanchia had just emptied her bank account to pay a quarterly instalment of the rates, and it would take stringent saving to manage the other three instalments.

She set her jaw. Once she began negotiating with the council she should be able to come to some agreement about any charges due.

'I know,' she said coldly. 'Do you want wit-
nesses to my signature?'

'Not unless you do—it's not a will.' A long,
lean-fingered hand offered a silver pen.

Accepting it, she ignored the jump in her
heart-rate when their fingers touched. Caid
waited until the pen had almost reached the
paper to say, 'And of course I trust you.'

Sanchia signed and dated the option with
slashing writing that came close to expressing
her chaotic emotions. 'There,' she said, drop-
ping the pen on the desk, 'although you bought
it dearly, even for a dollar.'

'I like to cover all bases,' Caid told her with
a flinty, level glance that set alarm bells jan-
gling. He folded the paper and dropped it onto
the dark polished surface of the desk.
Unsmiling, his eyes too calculating, he ushered
her towards the door. 'Can I get you something
to drink? You look a little hot.'

No doubt her face was scarlet. Resisting the
urge to moisten lips still tender from his kisses,
she said quietly, 'No, thank you. I'll head back
home now.'

'Of course.' Now that he'd got his worthless
option he'd retreated behind a mask of polite
indifference.

Sanchia walked beside him down the wide, airy hall and out onto the terrace that ran across the entire sea-front of the house. Bordered by a stone balustrade with wrought-iron infills, the charming terrace was a clever salute to Mrs Hunter's European heritage. Yet both house and terrace fitted into the splendid, entirely New Zealand surroundings.

'I'll go back by the beach,' Sanchia said, heading towards the cliff path. 'Don't come with me; I know the way.'

But he insisted on walking her down the twisting, narrow path beneath the trees, and along the beach to the boundary fence that ran back from the sand.

Stopping there, he tilted Sanchia's unwilling, defiantly composed face with a deft, strong hand beneath her chin. 'An affair between us wouldn't be sordid, either. Cosmic sounds much more like it.'

And he kissed her again, holding her still with not ungentle hands in her hair.

This kiss had all the flash and fire of the other, but added to it was something else even more dangerous—a seducing sweetness that stole Sanchia's wits and checked her instinctive fear for long, betraying moments.

Yet when it was over she growled, 'I meant every word I said about selling.'

'So,' he returned pleasantly—if she discounted the fine underpinning of steel to every word, 'did I.' He dropped his hands and stood back.

Routed and temporarily without an answer, Sanchia kept her face turned away while she walked away from him along the brazen beach, the sensitive hollow between her shoulderblades informing her that Caid watched her until she disappeared into the welcome shade of the pohutukawa trees.

Thrumming with adrenalin, she poured a glass of water from the jug in the refrigerator, but only drank half of it before she plonked the glass down and strode through the living room of the bach onto the deck, ferociously creating cutting, witty answers she could have flung at him.

You're making too much of the whole thing! she finally told herself sternly. He tried to soften you up, that's all. And even if he does want you, that means nothing. Men can want women they hate. So stop being an idiot! She dropped into an elderly wicker chair, only to leap out of it immediately. 'Ouch!'

She sprang out again and peered at the ragged hole in the seat before twisting to examine the scratches on her leg where the broken wickerwork had attacked her.

Her aunt's favourite chair; it had sat too long out in the weather. Swallowing hard, Sanchia went inside to dab the thin line of blood with antiseptic.

'All he did was kiss you,' she muttered, turning on the tap over the sink to make a cup of tea. Watching several drops sputter out, she said loudly, 'Just a kiss. Well, two kisses. Nothing important. You've been kissed before and liked it and this was no different.'

She lied. Cosmic, Caid had said. Trust him to choose exactly the right word. That first kiss had rocketed her out of her settled, placid existence and spun her into unknown realms of sensation.

And the second one had simply reinforced her complete inability to deal with him. Caid had kissed her with a fierce, potent sexuality that had scared her witless, yet she'd kissed him back with all the subtlety of a lioness in heat.

Impatiently she wrenched the uncooperative tap off and on again. 'Come on, water!'

But no stream of rainwater emerged, and the pump whined and spluttered before settling into a monotonous moan from its cupboard in the laundry.

'Oh, no!' The pump was notorious for misbehaving, and it would be difficult and horribly expensive to get a tradesman out during the holiday season.

Thumping the kettle down, she raced into the laundry and opened the cupboard to peer suspiciously inside. Apart from its irritating whine the pump seemed perfectly normal, without any signs of haemorrhaging oil or water.

Sanchia tried every other tap in the bach, a fruitless exercise. Unable to get up to pressure, the pump continued to labour with ominous persistence until she turned it off at the switch.

The only reason she could think of for the pump's failure to deliver water was so scary she had to force herself out to the large, circular concrete tank behind the bach. Armed with the long-handled broom, she tapped from the top of the tank to the bottom, the same hollow clunk, clunk, clunk all the way down confirming her worst fears.

No water.

And, once she looked for it, the reason was obvious. The guttering around the far side of the bach had rusted away, diverting all the precious rain of spring onto the ground. Last time Sanchia had stayed she'd been using water that couldn't be replenished.

'Let's not panic here,' she said out loud. 'It's a nuisance, but it isn't the end of the world. The electricity's still on and the gas bottle's more than half full. Buy some water.'

But she'd had the telephone disconnected. And she'd have to find out how much water cost; her bank account was too anorexic to be able to deal with more than a few dollars.

Of course, there was always her credit card.

'So find out how much a tanker-load of water costs, Sanchia,' she said aloud into the humid, unresponsive air.

Normally she'd have gone to the caretaker's flat behind the big house and asked to use their telephone, but the prospect of meeting Caid again set her skin prickling.

All right then, she'd walk to the farm manager's cottage.

After replenishing her sunscreen, she clapped on a wide-brimmed straw hat and set off for the Henleys' house, a beautifully renovated old farmhouse a couple of bays along.

It took her half an hour—thirty minutes of watching nervously for Caid Hunter to gallop over a hill on a gleaming black stallion like something from a fairy story. Except that in fairy stories the prince always arrived on a white horse, she thought with a wry smile.

But then Caid was no prince, no romantic stereotype. In the world of fairy tales he might even be the villain—devious, impossibly handsome, a little brutal.

And determined.

'Of course you can use the phone,' Pat's wife told her when Sanchia got there, hot and sticky and puffing slightly. 'I'll make some coffee while you're doing it.'

She even gave Sanchia the number of the tanker owner, whose wife wasn't nearly so welcoming. 'Do you know how many people

have used up all their water already?' she
asked wearily. 'Brett's working fifteen hours a
day trying to keep up with the demand. Where
did you say you are? Oh, Waiora Bay. Well,
there's no way we could get our tanker down
that hill. The corners are too sharp.'

Sanchia felt sick. Without water she'd have
to go back to Auckland. Until then she hadn't
realised how much she'd banked on this final
holiday to give her some sort of closure.
Compulsively rolling a pen back and forth,
back and forth, she asked, 'What about a small
tanker?'

'We haven't got one,' the woman said, mar-
ginally more sympathetic. 'You could try
Kerikeri—or even Kaitaia—but I don't think
either of them have one either, and they're
busy too. It's been a dry spring and summer
all over the north.'

'I see,' Sanchia said woodenly. 'Thanks
very much.'

'Look, I'll take your number—'

'I'm sorry, I don't have a phone.'

From the kitchen Molly Henley called,
'Give her our number, Sanchia.'

Gratefully Sanchia did so, and the other woman took it down, but warned, 'I can't promise anything.'

'I know. Thanks very much.'

'Bummer,' Molly commiserated when she'd hung up. 'Come and have your coffee while we work out what to do next.'

Things didn't seem quite so bad when Sanchia was sitting out on the verandah with a mug of coffee in her hand, feet propped up on the balustrade, the sun pouring onto a sea as blue and tender as a Madonna's robe.

Her hostess said practically, 'Caid had a bore put in for us so we've got plenty of water. Wait until Pat comes back—he'll work out some way of transporting it to the bach. Now, tell me what you've been doing since we saw you last.'

'Just the usual,' Sanchia said lightly. 'What have *you* been up to?'

Molly embarked on a funny, racy overview of district gossip, then asked, 'Have you seen Caid yet? He got in yesterday.'

'Yes.' Sanchia fiddled with the handle of her mug. 'Is his mother coming?'

'Haven't heard. I hope so; I like her. She's a bit stately—I think she finds us Kiwis really casual—but she's lovely. And she always brings presents for the children; nothing expensive, just thoughtfully chosen. I suspect she wants grandchildren.' Molly gave a comfortable laugh. 'She might have a wait on her hands because Caid doesn't seem ready to settle down yet. I know he doesn't turn up much in the newspapers, but I did read a snip about him and a high-powered magazine editor last year, and did you see the photo of him with that film star? Leila Sherif? She looked besotted. I wonder if she'll be here this summer.'

Repressing a snake-slither of jealousy, Sanchia said, 'Perhaps.' She had no right to be jealous.

'She won't if Mrs Hunter's coming,' Molly decided. 'He doesn't usually bring his girl-friends when his mother's in residence. Rather old-fashioned and nice of him, when you think of it.'

'He might be scared of her,' Sanchia suggested frivolously.

'Oh, for sure,' Molly scoffed, laughing. 'I can just see him shivering in his handmade shoes when she frowns at him. He's no mummy's boy. You didn't know his father, did you?'

'No.'

'Well, Caid's a real chip off the old block—tough as they come but fair with it. A good boss, although he gets his money's worth. I suppose he'll get married one day, but I doubt if it will be to please his mother.'

'Not many men do that,' Sanchia said drily, and steered the conversation to her hostess's children, a topic Molly indulged to the full with a willing listener.

A few minutes later Pat arrived. When Molly had explained Sanchia's predicament he said, 'Caid told me to keep an eye on the bach and I've checked it out regularly, but I never thought to look at the guttering. Yeah, I can take some water across on the tractor—I've got a forty-four gallon drum that'll do the job.'

'Thanks very much.' Sanchia smiled gratefully. 'It won't be too much trouble for you?'

'Not a problem. No need for you to head back to Auckland.' He made it sound as though she was planning to return to Sodom. 'I'll go and fill the drum now.' He winked at her. 'If you've finished gossiping, I'll give you a ride back on the tractor. Save you from another long, hot walk.'

Half an hour later Sanchia was perched on the tray of the tractor, laughing as she anchored her hat to her head—laughter that was cut off abruptly by a short toot from behind. She swivelled to see Caid at the wheel of an elderly Land Rover.

So much, she thought feverishly, for her character analysis—this vehicle was about as far as you could get from a Lamborghini! Pat's tractor was newer and more luxurious.

Obeying the unspoken command, Pat pulled into the side of the road and switched off the engine. The Land Rover eased to a stop and Caid got out. He was not smiling.

Sanchia's heart gave a peculiar leap in her breast.

'What are you doing?' he asked, his glance not leaving her face.

She felt as though she'd been branded for life by that intent, unsparing regard. 'Getting a ride home,' she told him in a voice spiked with antagonism.

Uncompromising blue eyes switched to Pat. 'It's illegal to take a passenger on a tractor.'

Sanchia protested, 'It's as safe as a quad,' referring to the sturdy little four-wheeled vehicles, a cross between a motorbike and a tiny tractor, that had become a farming workhorse.

'You're not supposed to carry passengers on quads, either. Pat?' Caid said with a quiet authority that demanded an answer.

Pat tipped his hat back on his head. 'We're sticking to the road, Caid, not heading over the hills. She's pretty safe.'

Caid's expression didn't alter. 'Sanchia, I'll give you a ride home.'

She wasn't going to brawl with him in front of Pat, who didn't deserve any trouble with his employer, especially as technically Pat was in the wrong. So, although she made no attempt to hide the animosity glittering in her eyes and avoided Caid's outstretched hand, she jumped down from the tray and said over her shoulder, 'There's not so much dust in his Land Rover, Pat.'

Pat winked. 'I'll see you at the bach, then.'

Ignoring Caid, she clambered into the Land Rover and gazed deliberately around the cab;

spartan the vehicle might be, but it was well-maintained. She let her gaze slip through the windscreen and saw Caid say something to Pat, who grinned as he replied with a quick gesture. Caid flung back his black head and laughed.

No, she thought in anguish. I can't bear this all over again. Three years ago she'd cut him from her life with ruthless, single-minded determination; instinct warned her that if she let him get too close this time, she'd be left with more than a badly scarred heart.

When he turned to get into the car his face was almost grim, the angular features hard and inflexible. Fine, she could deal with that.

He closed the door behind him with a control that jolted her nerves, then drove past the tractor slowly so the manager didn't get showered in dust.

'Home?' he asked, his polite tone setting her teeth on edge.

'Yes, thank you.' She paused, then said, 'I know it's illegal to take passengers on a tractor, and I can understand that no one should ever carry children, but—'

'If you're trying to make sure I don't sack Pat you can stop right now,' Caid interrupted in a steely voice. 'He won't be carrying passengers again, and he's too good a man to lose to the enticement of sultry green eyes and a sexy smile.'

Sanchia opened her mouth, then snapped it shut on the words that jostled on the tip of her tongue.

Caid said, 'And don't tell me he's old enough to be your father or that he dandled you on his knee when you were a baby. He'd have to be dead not to respond to you.'

'I'll bet you say that to all the girls,' she said sardonically.

His mouth tightened. They drove in simmering silence until they reached the bach. Once they were both out of the car Caid looked at the tank. 'What happened?'

'You can see where the guttering is rusted through.'

His brows drew together as he surveyed the results of her great-aunt's neglect. 'Get your clothes. You can stay at the house.'

'Of course I can't,' Sanchia snapped. 'Molly has visitors arriving this afternoon. I'll manage with the water Pat's delivering—we used to have problems with water every summer so I know how to be careful with it.'

He looked at her as though she were a madwoman. 'My house, Sanchia, not Pat and Molly's.'

How to deal with this? Too swiftly she returned, 'That's a very kind offer, but...' biting back the conventional thanks when he smiled mockingly at her. Sanchia ground her teeth together until she'd regained enough composure to finish, 'And I doubt whether your mother would be happy to find an uninvited guest in residence when she arrives.'

Broad shoulders lifted in a shrug. 'Why not? She likes you,' he said casually, 'and she's the most hospitable woman I know. Why don't you give me the real reason?'

Sheer panic drove her to say blindly, 'If you already know it why should I bother?'

To the sound of the tractor emerging from the bush he said satirically, 'You'd be quite safe. You have my word on it.'

Safe? Common sense told her that he was probably using his charm as a weapon to persuade her to sell the Bay—but common sense was no defence against kisses that had the power to steal her heart from her breast.

As though she'd spoken the words out loud he added, 'As safe as you want to be.'

She breathed deeply. 'Are you daring me?'

His laugh held more of a taunt than a challenge. 'I grew out of that when I was about fourteen. Would it take so much courage to spend a few nights in my house?'

'None at all,' she said coolly, 'if it was necessary. But it's not, because here's Pat with enough water to keep me going for quite a while. He said he'd deliver some more if I run out. Provided you give your permission,' she added.

'Of course he can,' Caid said curtly.

The tractor drew up with a flourish and Pat leaned down. 'Where do you want the drum?' he called above the engine.

'As close to the house as possible, thank you.'

Pat backed the tractor up to the house and lowered the tray; he leapt down and helped Caid slide the drum onto the ground.

Sanchia tried very hard to keep her eyes on the older man, but once again she couldn't help noting the play of muscles as Caid used his long arms and strong shoulders to manoeuvre the drum of water off the tray and into position.

When it was in place he turned too quickly, catching her widening gaze. Something flared in his eyes; his mouth set into a fixed humourless smile.

Skin prickling, she dragged her gaze away. He knew—but then he'd known how vulnerable she was to him the moment she'd gone up in flames under his sorcerous, knowledgeable kiss.

He was far too astute not to start asking questions if she kept on responding so—so feverishly to him and then flinched away. And too astute not to come up with something like the truth. The cold emptiness in the centre of her stomach expanded into barely controlled panic.

She couldn't bear it if he ever found out why she couldn't stand a man's hands on her.

Moving into his house would be the most idiotic thing she could do. And not only stupid—very, very dangerous, because she was so aware of him that she sensed the first slippery approach to that terrifying roller-coaster called love.

After satisfying himself that she could easily get water from the drum, Caid left with another of those slashing smiles, all edge and aggression and flagrant male anticipation—the kind of smile sensible women fled from.

Gnawed by a foolish, bitter resentment, Sanchia waved Pat off, then slammed inside and pulled on her bathing suit. Although faded, it would last her out this summer. And it suited her—the soft rose lent some colour to her pale arms and legs.

Swimming did nothing to ease the clutch of foreboding; it tightened as she sat out on the deck with a book she'd been trying to read for several weeks. After a few minutes she made a sharp, disgusted sound and closed the pages on words that had wavered and shifted, forming into meaningless patterns.

She'd expected trouble from Caid when he found she wasn't going to sell the Bay; what she hadn't expected was to be ambushed by a charged, sexual rush every time she saw him.

If only she'd been able to hide it.

Ha! She didn't have a hope in Hades of controlling it, and he was too experienced not to know what happened whenever he touched her, kissed her. Damn him, he knew that her breasts tightened, knew all about the slow, reckless ache of desire in her loins...

Her insides clamped into a delicious knot. Jerkily, she twisted out of the chair and fled inside.

A breeze flirted in through the open doors, tumbling the Christmas cards on the bookshelves into a tinselly crimson and green scatter across the floor. Grateful for the distraction, she picked them up. She'd brought them because she'd hoped they'd make the bach festive, but they were past their season and merely looked tired, so she dropped them in the rubbish bin.

Restlessness prowled through her veins. Perhaps she should go and get the paper from the mailbox.

'Too hot,' she said out loud. She'd go in the evening when it was cooler. Setting her jaw, she took some stationery from her bag and sat at the table to write letters.

An hour and some stiff pages later, tension drove her into her aunt's bedroom. Everything had gone except the furniture and a pile of old magazines on the bookshelf. The echoing emptiness of the small room chilled her; she turned away at the door and went into her own bedroom to pick up the little wooden box of papers she'd promised herself she'd go through. It had travelled down to Auckland with her, lain untouched in her bedroom there, and come back. She couldn't bear to open it and paw through her great-aunt's life.

When she looked at the marquetry pattern on the lid tears ached behind her eyes. She put the box away again and went out onto the terrace, collapsing into the chair.

Time had never dragged when Great-Aunt Kate was alive. And it certainly didn't drag when she was with Caid.

Sanchia forced herself to finish the letters.

In the cool of the evening she walked down to the gate on the coastal road and collected the paper from the mailbox. Back at the bach she read it with a total lack of interest before finally taking herself off to bed.

The next day was even hotter. After lunch Sanchia went for her third swim, but this time when she walked out of the water it was to see Caid striding towards her, a dark, powerful figure in the solemn shade of the pohutukawas. Awareness and a taut, breathless anticipation jolted through her; she'd been waiting for him.

No, she thought, and, even more strongly, No!

This humiliating weakness tore her determination to shreds. She and Caid Hunter were at opposite ends of the scale—he was rich and powerful; she was poor and powerless—and in spite of the attraction that set her aflame when he looked at her she'd never be able to give him the sexual surrender he expected.

For her own peace of mind—for any sort of future—she had to get rid of him. Attack was the best method of defence, and if ever she'd needed to defend herself, now was the time.

Without trying to hide her frown, she reached for the towel she'd hung over a branch and draped it around her shoulders. Aggressively, she demanded, 'What do you want?'

CHAPTER FOUR

NO MUSCLES moved in Caid's face, but Sanchia sensed a hardening, an inflexible concentration of attention on her as he replied, 'I don't like to see you swimming by yourself— it's too risky. I know you're a strong swimmer, but even strong swimmers can find themselves in trouble.'

She shrugged. 'I'm very sensible. I don't go out too far or stay in too long, and I've never had cramp in my life.' With a thin smile she summoned an edge to her voice. 'If I drowned you'd probably be able to buy the Bay, so I'm rather ambivalent about your charming solicitude. I'll be all right, Caid. Go back to your big house and accept that for once you can't make someone do what you want.'

His lashes drooped. Sanchia grabbed a corner of her towel and wiped a trickle of water from the side of her face. He still hadn't moved; he stood watching her with a faint smile on his handsome face, yet she felt his anger as if it were the pulsing red aura some people claimed to see.

'But, Sanchia, we both know I *can* make you do exactly what I want,' he drawled, his voice low and smooth and deadly.

Hot humiliation engulfed her. Forcing her chin upwards, she met his gaze with defiance. 'If you think a few kisses are enough to sweeten—'

Caustic, calculating, he cut her off. 'Waiora Bay is not yours to do with as you wish.'

Her hand stilled. Clutching the damp fold of towel so that it hid the lower part of her face, she stared at him with widening eyes. 'What on earth do you mean?'

Hard, intimidating, his gaze held hers. 'Obviously you don't know that for the past six years I've been paying your great-aunt an annuity on the understanding that when she died I had the right to buy the property.'

Whatever she'd expected, it wasn't this. Shaking her head, Sanchia said numbly, 'I don't believe you.'

'I don't lie,' he told her, each word brutal with decision.

The towel dropped from her limp fingers; she made an odd pushing gesture with her hands, repudiating his monstrous statement. Words stumbled out, slowly at first, and then faster and more intemperate, slashing through the warm, heavy air like rapiers. 'Why would she have done that? She didn't need your money.'

She was going to blurt out her great-aunt's plans for the Bay: she could feel the words building on her tongue and had to swallow them, whip up anger to stop them bursting forth. 'Is that how you've got where you are— with dirty tricks and dishonesty?'

'I have proof.' He spoke with uncompromising authority, his reasonable tone at variance with his eyes, cold and compelling beneath their thick lashes.

Another vehement shake of Sanchia's head sent wet snakes of hair flying around her face. She fought a bitter anger and an even more bitter disillusionment. 'Great-Aunt Kate would sooner have cut off her hand than sell the Bay.'

Anger prowled behind his controlled façade. 'Your great-aunt wrote to me and suggested the annuity. I have the documents, signed by her. She had no right to leave this place to you without telling you about this.'

'That's a lie.' Dismissing him with contempt, she turned away.

'If you were a man,' he said in a voice that froze her witless, 'you'd learn not to toss accusations like that at me.'

Dry-mouthed, she counter-attacked, 'But it's perfectly all right for you to accuse Great-Aunt Kate of cheating! When you offered to buy the Bay from me there was no talk of any annuity. Why didn't you mention it then?'

Why indeed? It was a question Caid had no intention of answering—mainly because he didn't have a logical reason. In fact, since Sanchia had arrived at the Bay he'd carefully avoided facing the implications of his unusual behaviour.

He said evenly, 'I offered you a conservative price for the Bay, a price that took in the amount of money I'd already paid Miss Tregear. The annuity was an agreement between your great-aunt and me, and I respected her privacy.'

Of course she wouldn't leave it there; he hadn't expected her to. For a fleeting moment

he wondered what it would be like to claim all
her infuriating, inconvenient loyalty, to know
that whatever happened she'd be there for him,
as his mother had been for his father. He'd
never expected such loyalty from any of the
women he'd liked and wooed and bedded;
he'd treated them with consideration and respect, but he'd steered well clear of commit-
ment.

So it probably served him right that he still
wanted the woman who'd fled from him like
a deer chased by wolves.

Great green eyes smouldering with suspicion, her luscious mouth thin, Sanchia demanded, 'What about the option?' Her eyes
narrowed. 'You *were* testing me! You thought
I'd jump at the offer of a few thousand. Is it
just me you despise, or do you think all women
are greedy cheats?'

He made a noise that could have been scorn
or frustration, or a mixture of both. 'Go and
get dressed,' he commanded. 'Then perhaps
we can discuss this like adults instead of shouting at each other.'

Taut, determined to make him see the truth,
she said, 'The day before Great-Aunt Kate

died she talked for over an hour about her hopes for the Bay. She wanted to safeguard the bush and the pohutukawas—the butterfly tree especially—make sure no developers could ever spoil the Bay. Caid, these trees have *names*!' She pointed to each one, giving their names in the melodious Maori language. 'No one alive knows what they refer to, but these trees played their parts in battles and love affairs, in feuds and trysts and peace-making marriages. They're living history. I promised Great-Aunt Kate I wouldn't ever sell the Bay, and I simply can't believe that she'd make an agreement with you.'

His hard-honed features remained impassive. 'And I can't believe she demanded such a promise from you when she had no right. Unless she was—'

'She wasn't crazy! She was as sharp on the day she died as she'd ever been!'

'I didn't say anything about her being crazy.' He reined in his impatience.

Sanchia set off for the bach, pausing just long enough to fling at him, 'I consider her wishes for the Bay to be a sacred trust.'

'An expensive sacred trust,' Caid observed, the comment an indolent taunt.

Although he walked behind her, she felt him with an awareness that was like sight and touch together, a primitive consciousness rooted in the genes.

Ignoring it, Sanchia strode through the clinging grass towards the bach. Steadily, icily, she said, 'Your implication that she asked for money is outrageous.'

'I'm not *implying* that she asked for it,' he shot back, 'I'm *telling* you.'

He had to be lying.

And that, Sanchia thought, hit by an inchoate sense of loss, was unexpectedly painful. Why should she care that Caid Hunter was unscrupulous? Or even be surprised?

Cold disdain stiffened her spine, braced her resolve. 'There is no reason for her to do that.'

'She wrote to me about it the year you went to university. Look out!'

Too late. Sanchia cannoned into the pillar that supported the verandah over the deck. Although she managed to jerk sideways, and so avoid hitting it fair and square, the blow sent her staggering and drove all the breath from her body.

Caid grabbed her. 'Are you hurt?' he asked, his voice thick and fast and angry. A lean finger pushed her chin up and he scanned her face intently for bruises.

'My pride is,' she muttered. She wrenched out of his grasp, clutching the sun-warmed post while she tried to regain some composure.

He asked, 'Do you make a habit of walking into things?'

'Not normally.' Only when she was with him. His gaze dropped, then flicked up again, and she realised that the strap of her bathing suit had slipped down her arm, revealing the white curve of one small breast. Yanking it up, she said, 'I'm all right.'

'Get dressed,' he said brusquely.

Her aunt's stringent training in hospitality persuaded her to say with equal brevity, 'Be careful how you sit down—some of the chairs have perished,' before she walked into the bach.

Seething, she headed for the bathroom. Once she got there, however, she glowered at the bucket of water beside the handbasin; it seemed significant—an omen, even—hinting at how easily things could go wrong.

Not, she thought fiercely, this time. Whatever threats Caid came up with, she'd make sure she carried out her last promise to her great-aunt.

After she'd wriggled free of her wet bathing suit she checked herself in the mirror, tentatively touching a welt along one cheekbone. It could have been worse.

Thank Mother Nature or evolution for quick reflexes, she thought sardonically, as she sponged herself with a couple of inches of lukewarm water in the bottom of the basin. Trying not to recall just how rapidly Caid had grabbed her, she dried off as much as she could of the salt and sunscreen clinging to her skin.

Had Great-Aunt Kate approached Caid about an annuity because Sanchia had needed the money to go to university? There had never been any discussion about it; it had always been a given.

No. If she'd done that she would have told Sanchia. He had to be lying.

The quick wash cooled her down, helped her feel a little more able to deal with the man waiting for her. Her face setting into determined severity, she slipped on a loose shift in clear silvery green, combed her hair straight back and walked outside.

Motionless, patient, Caid was staring out to sea, radiating a coiled intensity that was a warning. He couldn't have heard the soft whisper of her bare feet, but he turned as she came towards the doors, dark face aloof and watchful.

He had the instincts, the keen awareness of every predator. Before he could speak she demanded, 'What proof do you have of this supposed deal?'

His smile revealed too many white teeth. 'Letters. The agreement. Signed by both of us.'

'Where's the agreement?'

Caid looked at her with eyes half-concealed by his heavy lids. 'In my Auckland office.'

Sanchia lifted her brows. 'Of course,' she murmured with cutting politeness. 'What a pity it's the holidays. I don't suppose there's anyone in your office now who can post it up.'

'It's being faxed through now,' he said negligently. 'And why don't you look in your great-aunt's papers? If the agreement didn't go to the solicitor dealing with her estate, you must find her copy of it here. Provided nothing's happened to it.'

The implication wasn't lost on Sanchia. 'I can promise you I haven't burnt it,' she said. Stony-faced, she swung on her heels and strode into her aunt's bedroom. One hand hefted the marquetry box; she carried it out and unlocked it, then tipped the contents onto the rickety table against the wall. The westering sun sneaked in beneath the verandah roof and smouldered across her bare skin as she flicked through the small pile of papers.

'Birth certificates,' she snapped, pushing a long envelope to one side after a cursory glance. 'Her passport. My school reports. Some extremely old letters in a rubber band. Nothing else—and her other papers went to the solicitor. I'm sure he'd have noticed if there'd been any sort of agreement to sell the Bay. Just as I'm certain Great-Aunt Kate would have told me if she'd known about such a thing.'

Her hands shook slightly as she slapped the papers back in the box and turned the key in the padlock. 'Nothing,' she repeated, and turned to face Caid. 'Unless you can show me an agreement with her signature, then I'm afraid I can't believe you.'

He covered the distance between them in two long strides and grasped her shoulders. His fingers didn't tighten but she froze. Green eyes clashed with blue, neither giving nor demanding quarter.

His mouth hard, his tone silkily menacing, he said, 'When the fax comes through I expect to be able to discuss some sort of deal with you.'

He waited, and when she said nothing he went on more gently, 'It's no use, Sanchia. I have the documents. I admire your loyalty to your great-aunt, but I'm afraid she didn't deserve it.'

Sanchia called on her will-power and took a difficult step backwards, removing herself from the influence of that deep voice, those intensely-coloured eyes, that overwhelming aura of beautiful, dangerous masculinity.

Angry, strangely hurt, Sanchia gave way to a treacherous urge to explain why she had to fulfil her great-aunt's last wish. 'She deserved it. She saved my life.'

'How?'

He spoke lazily, almost indifferently, but she sensed his interest. Regretting the impulse to confide, she said quietly, 'She rescued me from an—from hell.'

His brows drew together. Quick and savage, he demanded, 'What sort of hell?'

Sanchia shrugged and resisted the temptation to go any further. He used those pauses like weapons, and she wasn't going to fall for it again. 'Just a bad scene,' she said woodenly.

'I'm glad she saved you,' he said, and it was impossible to tell whether he believed her melodramatic statement or not, 'but she extracted a hundred and twenty thousand dollars from me while apparently not intending to follow through on her legal obligations. Not only that, but she put you in an untenable position.'

Sanchia picked up Great-Aunt Kate's box and headed into the house. 'She'd never have lied to me,' she said coldly over her shoulder. 'Not even by omission.' She stopped in the doorway, her eyes opaque and dismissive. 'Goodbye, Mr Hunter. Get off my land before I have you thrown off for trespass and harassment.'

To her astonishment he laughed. Nonplussed and insulted, Sanchia stared haughtily at him.

Something gleamed in the depths of his eyes. 'I should ask you to work for me,' he said. 'I could make use of that splendid arrogance.'

Was that a hint of a bribe, an offer of a job in his organisation if she sold the land to him? 'Thank you, but I'm perfectly happy in my present job.'

He'd been watching her, but his attention suddenly shifted. Looking past her, he asked sharply, 'What's that smell?'

'I don't—' But she too could smell it now.

'Gas,' he said, and surged towards her in a silent, ferocious rush, half-carrying, half-forcing her out of the bach.

By the time he pushed her face-down onto the grass behind the concrete tank her chest was heaving and her blood drumming in her ears. His weight pinned her to the ground as he rolled slightly, manoeuvring her so that he shielded her with his big body, covering her entirely, his long legs clamping hers. Gasping, she gave way to the panic surging icily through her.

'Stop struggling, damn you,' Caid commanded, holding her still with carefully controlled strength.

Sanchia dammed the scream that threatened to tear her vocal chords, repeating like a mantra that this was Caid, who had never hurt her...

'Are you all right?' he asked suddenly, and in an instant she was free, able to roll over onto her back and take in deep, shuddering breaths.

Forcing her breath evenly through her lips, she relaxed every tense muscle and flung her arm up over her eyes, concentrating with every shred of self-possession she could muster on the reason for that suspicious, frightening trace of gas.

'Sanchia, answer me!'

Wetting her lips, she croaked, 'I'm fine. Just a bit winded—I didn't expect you to fling me down like that.' Hastily she changed the subject. 'There must be a gas leak—perhaps it's a loose connection to the stove.'

There was a tight moment of silence before he said grimly, 'Your great-aunt obviously let things go—that guttering didn't rust away overnight, or even in the past six months. And if the gas bottle is damaged, or just too old, the bach could blow up any minute.'

'My car,' she said, wrenching her arm away from her eyes to stare into a face so harshly outlined she blinked. The emotion—rage?— that darkened his eyes vanished, replaced by the usual vivid opacity.

He caught her hand and held it firmly. 'You're not going anywhere near the bach.'

'I need that car, and it's parked within six feet of the gas bottle!'

'It's too risky. In this heat, starting a car could provide enough of a spark to send the place up,' he said harshly. Lean fingers slid from her wrist to her elbow, supporting her as she hauled herself upwards. 'Better the car than you.'

Furiously, helplessly, she snapped, 'So what do I do, then?'

His eyes dropped to the smooth expanse of leg exposed by her rucked-up shift; white-lipped, Sanchia tugged the material down to cover her thighs.

'I know danger is supposed to act as an aphrodisiac, but it doesn't with me,' he drawled. 'You're quite safe. I'll collect those papers—you might need them later. Stay here.' He set off towards the bach.

Assaulted by a complex mixture of emotions, Sanchia scrambled to her feet; before she'd taken two steps after him he swung around and demanded savagely, 'Do I have to tie you to a bloody tree with my belt?'

'If it's safe enough for you to go in there it's safe enough for me.'

'And if I need to run for it you'll be in the way,' he retorted roughly.

'I'd rather the bach and the car went up in flames...' She stopped, then said with a wry smile, 'Or, as you put it, better the car and the bach than you. And you'll have a real problem on your hands if you try to tie me to a tree.'

She was no match for him and they both knew it. His eyes narrowed. 'In that case we'll leave now and go up to the house. I'll organise someone who knows what they're doing to check it out.'

Sanchia dragged her gaze away from his to stare at a clump of agapanthus, blue and white starbursts of flowers poised like huge dandelion heads above the strappy leaves. Her conversation with the tanker driver's wife in her mind, she said, 'It's not likely you'll get anyone to come during the holidays.'

'Of course I will,' he said with such confidence that she blinked.

'Well, naturally,' she drawled. 'For Caid Hunter, any expert would drop everything to come running!'

He shrugged, but ignored the snide little remark. 'Come on, we'll go home. I don't think there's any immediate danger of the gas exploding, but the further away we are the safer I'll feel.'

'Me too,' she said with a shiver.

Keeping the bulk of the bach between them and the gas bottle, Caid set off so fast her long legs struggled to keep up with him. Although she knew it was almost certainly safe, Sanchia could hear her heart beating in her eardrums, and halfway along the hot sand she rubbed eyes that were unaccountably blurred, then fished out her handkerchief and blew her nose.

'What's the matter?' Caid asked instantly.

'Nothing.' But her voice cracked on the word and she couldn't stop shivering.

'You're shocked,' he said roughly, and she was abruptly enfolded in warmth, held against a lean body, safe in strong arms. 'My blood runs cold when I think you could have been killed any time since you arrived here.'

His hooded blue gaze met hers. Her breath blocked her throat as he bent his head, and her body refused to obey her urgent signals to get the hell out of there.

She even lifted her face to his, shivering at the flash of triumph she saw there. And then he kissed her and she was lost in the dark enchantment his mouth wreaked, in a world where the only thing that mattered was the male scent in her nostrils, the pressure of his mouth on hers, the hot, lithe power of the body against hers.

Sensation—piercingly sweet yet languorous, dangerously decadent—poured through her, sapping her will-power, driving her with the delicate lash of sexuality towards an erotic trap.

Gasping, she tried to pull away, and Caid took swift, expert advantage, probing into the tender depths. Sanchia had no way of controlling the electricity that melted her bones and heated the exquisitely sensitive area between her thighs.

Through the humming in her ears she heard a low, stifled groan; horrified, she realised that it came from her own throat. And almost immediately the black panic surged up from its hiding place deep in her psyche, and she began to struggle.

His arms dropped from around her. Watching her closely, he asked, 'What's the matter?'

Was that amusement in his voice, in the curve of his mouth? She'd never been able to read him. Green eyes glittering, lips clamped in a humiliating mixture of fear and frustration, she muttered, 'It was just reaction.'

'Was it?' he asked, blue eyes probing. 'Reaction to what?'

Sanchia took an involuntary step backwards. 'The prospect of being blown up in a gas explosion, of course.' She tried for a coolly dismissive stare before stiffening her sinews and forcing one foot in front of the other.

Without comment Caid strode along beside her.

More than anything in this world she wanted to go back to the bach, pack up and flee to the safety of Auckland. Instead she couldn't even think; her brains rattled loosely around her head.

Loose. Oh, yes, that was the right word. Shameless, loose, wanton…

And then the hideous kick of terror. Nothing had changed.

Once in the house Caid installed her in a chair with a glass of heavily sugared lime juice before ringing the fire brigade.

As he spoke he saw Sanchia's hands curve around the glass as though seeking comfort from it. Nausea hollowed his stomach. She could have been killed in an inferno—all that beauty, her lively mind, her tart tongue, that indefinable appeal blown away in a senseless accident.

A few concise explanations later, his gaze drifted back to Sanchia. Her face was almost serene, if you could discount the faint shadows beneath her eyes, and the long fingers clasping the glass seemed still and relaxed; only the shimmer on top of the liquid gave her away.

Yet that impeccable control splintered whenever he touched her; each time he'd kissed her the erotic, sensual intensity of her response had been so arousing he'd had to stop himself from taking her luscious mouth up on the promises it made, making himself master of that elegant, slender body.

Until the barriers slammed into place. Why had she frozen beneath him on the grass, her green eyes blank with terror, then gone berserk?

Although she still wanted him with potent, sensuous passion, she was as unwilling as she had been three years previously. Mixed signals—and he was beginning to suspect the reason for them.

Dragging his attention back to the fire chief, he said grimly, 'All right, we'll wait for you to come and check it over. Thank you.'

Sanchia's green gaze lifted and fixed onto his face with painful intensity. 'What's happening?'

'They'll be out immediately. In the mean-time we're not to go anywhere near the bach.'

Her lashes fell. 'Well, no,' she said vaguely.

He said, 'Wait there,' and left the room.

Sanchia watched him go, her eyes dwelling with bitter appreciation on the breadth of his shoulders, the way he moved, all lithe male grace and alertness.

She took another sip of sweetly tart lime juice and cursed her susceptibility. Yet Caid wasn't just muscles and testosterone and that heart-twisting face; as well as high-handed and forceful and uncompromising, he'd been pro-tective and thoughtful and careful of her...

He came back through the doorway. Dark blue eyes checked her face. 'Are you all right?'

'Yes,' she said thinly. 'What's that?'

He paused, then said, 'It can wait.'

It was a faxed document. Her eyes flew to his, met an unreadable barrier of cobalt; she said, 'I'd like to see it now.'

After another searching glance he gave the sheets of paper to her; she looked down, and to her astonishment felt his hand on her shoul-der. Solid, warm, almost possessive, it stayed there.

Biting her lip, she bullied her mind to concentrate on the document.

It verified what he'd told her. Twenty thousand dollars was to be paid to Katherine Tregear each year until the agreed price had been reached or Katherine Tregear died, when any excess value of the land at Waiora Bay was to be paid to her estate. Caid's name was written in a slashing hand, saved from flamboyance by a disciplined control.

Sanchia's eyes rested on the other signature: 'Katherine Tregear'.

Sanchia closed her eyes for a moment. A violent mixture of relief and foreboding churned her stomach as she opened them again and focused on the date.

'That isn't Great-Aunt Kate's signature,' she said evenly.

CHAPTER FIVE

CAID'S fingers tightened only fractionally on her shoulder, yet when he let her go and stepped back Sanchia could feel the marks burning into her skin.

'How do you know she didn't sign it?' he asked with an unsettling detachment.

'Because her name was Kate.' She spelt it for him. 'Not Katherine.'

His dark brows drew together over his arrogant nose as he looked down at the faxed document with its forged signature. 'Kate is short for Katherine, surely?'

'Not in her case, and I can prove it,' she returned crisply. 'In fact, I can show you her birth certificate—it's in her box. Her father said that if they were going to call her Kate then Kate she'd be registered and Kate she'd be christened, so her legal name was Kate. She'd never have signed anything "Katherine".'

Sanchia was suddenly acutely aware of how big Caid was, how heavily muscled, of the difference between his hard strength and her slender litheness. He hadn't moved, hadn't even looked at her, yet she felt a primitive apprehension as strong as it was unexpected.

But when he spoke his voice was noncommittal, almost indifferent. 'Is that her writing?'

'It looks like it.' She felt sick. 'But it's not, Caid. After she died I had to give the funeral director her details for the death notice. He wanted to see the birth certificate. Her name was just Kate Tregear. Not even a second name; her father thought they were useless appendages.'

There was a significant silence. 'If this is true,' Caid said at last, his tone neutral, 'and your great-aunt did not initiate or sign this agreement, who did?'

'I don't know.' Someone who'd wanted twenty thousand dollars a year—someone who'd stolen a hundred and twenty thousand dollars from him. The amount buzzed in her head, ominous, terrifying.

Was Caid evil and deceitful enough to set up this scenario so she'd be forced to sell the Bay? Bile rose bitter in Sanchia's throat. It didn't seem possible, yet what did she know about him except that when he kissed her he stole her mind away, and that he was ruthless enough to run a huge and growing corporation?

And that he was capable of casual kindness.

Sanchia looked down at the papers in her hand; his signature wavered before her eyes. 'Was this all set up through intermediaries?'

'Yes. I was overseas, and she asked for discretion—pride, I thought. I understand pride.' He looked dispassionately at the fax sheets. 'The negotiations were all done by mail through the Auckland office. You say this wasn't signed by Kate Tregear, so clearly someone there didn't do a thorough enough check. I'll find out who that was.'

That was when Sanchia believed that he'd had nothing to do with the forgery. Her uneasy glance collided with a face of stone. Devoutly glad she wasn't that careless someone, she said, 'What will you do?'

'I'll get someone onto it right away—and they can start with the solicitor she used,' Caid said without expression.

'Not Mr Jameson.' Sanchia lifted her head sharply, eyes searching the hard angles of Caid's face. 'I might just conceive of Great-Aunt Kate being a party to fraud if she thought she had good enough reason, but the thought of Mr Jameson—who is elderly and fussy and the soul of rectitude—doing anything illegal is just plain ridiculous.'

'If your great-aunt didn't sign that deed, someone has stolen a considerable amount of money from me,' Caid said evenly. 'I intend to find out who that someone is and see that they get what they deserve.'

'Fair enough,' Sanchia said, setting her chin against a definite and chilling threat, 'just so long as you accept that it wasn't Great-Aunt Kate.'

'But who else,' he asked on a lethally reflective note, 'would have known enough about her to organise this?' He paused and added, 'Apart from you, of course.'

If he could make unpleasant insinuations, so could she; it was one thing to suspect, another entirely to be suspected. 'Why shouldn't the supposed annuity be transferred from one bank account to another, and used to give some-one—say, someone interested in buying the Bay—a whole lot of leverage to force that sale?'

She saw the anger leap into his eyes, and noted, with reluctant respect, his instant command of it. 'I don't lie and I don't cheat,' he said slowly, his heavy-lidded eyes never leaving her face. 'That bank account isn't mine and its account number will be in the records.'

'Would the bank tell you who owns it?' Sanchia was still bristling. 'New Zealand has a privacy act. Of course, you could find an unscrupulous hacker to go into their records…'

He shrugged, magnificently dismissive of any privacy act. 'Or go to the police.'

Sanchia resisted eyes so vividly saturated with blue it was impossible to see into their depths. His almost indifferent voice didn't hide the cold determination behind it. This time the threat was extremely personal.

Her hand shook as she put the papers down on the table beside her chair. Controlling a driving urgency to get out of there, to leave all this behind, she squared her shoulders and folded her hands in her lap, holding them still with stringent will-power.

'If you've lost that money to a forger I'm sorry,' she said steadily, 'but Great-Aunt Kate didn't sign that document, and I certainly didn't. So I don't feel I have even a moral responsibility.'

'I don't believe,' he said, still with that formidable self-assurance, 'I've implied any such thing.'

'Good.' Getting to her feet, she drew in a quick, furious breath and stared straight into his angular, impassive face as she finished, 'I'll see whether Great-Aunt Kate has any other papers—'

He broke in with a biting flash of temper. 'You're not going anywhere near that building until it's been checked and the source of the gas leak found and dealt with.'

'Oh—I'd forgotten.' Feeling foolish, Sanchia shifted her gaze to the document. Who had gone to those lengths? Someone who knew enough about Great-Aunt Kate to do it, who wanted money enough to forge a signature, someone who might even feel entitled to that money...

'What is it?' Caid demanded as she snatched up the papers and shuffled through them to stare at the signature.

'Nothing.' She said it too hastily.

'You've thought of someone?' When she didn't move or answer his voice hardened. 'Who?'

Silence stretched tautly between them until he probed, 'What was the name of this aunt you lived with after your parents died? The one you quarrelled with and ran away from before your great-aunt found you sleeping rough in a park and brought you here.'

'Cathy,' Sanchia mumbled.

'I'm sorry, I didn't hear you.'

'Catherine.' Her face rigid, she dropped the fax sheets with shaking fingers as though they contaminated her. 'But her name is spelt with a C, not a K.'

'Catherine Tregear?'

Hideous memories swirled through Sanchia. Controlling her face, her voice with an iron will, she said, 'Yes.'

Another of those tense, icy pauses. 'Where is she, this aunt Catherine of yours?'

'I don't know.' Sanchia took a shallow breath. 'I haven't seen her for years. We aren't close.'

Another understatement—so understated, in fact, that it came near to being a lie. Cathy Tregear hated her.

'How many years?'

Sanchia broke through the cage of her memories to say, 'Eleven. But why would she—?'

'I am,' he murmured, his eyes burning almost hypnotically, 'a strong believer in hunches. Isn't twenty thousand dollars a year reason enough? Was she mentioned in your great-aunt's will?'

'No,' Sanchia said stiffly.

'Unusual, surely? Why didn't Kate leave her a share of her estate?'

Sanchia rallied her wits. 'Why should she? Mr Jameson told me that sharing an ancestor with someone doesn't entitle you to a claim on their estate unless you're a child or grandchild. And as Cathy is only a niece of Great-Aunt Kate she has no claim to the Bay.'

'Waiora Bay is worth a lot of money,' Caid said cynically. 'If Cathy Tregear was told the same thing—that she had no claim—could she have conceived a method of getting what she might consider her rightful share? Fraud is simpler and less expensive than waiting to contest any will. What sort of person is she?'

'I don't really know.' At his narrow-eyed disbelief she added, 'I only lived with her for a couple of months.'

'What made you run away?'

White-faced, Sanchia said raggedly, 'I told you, we quarrelled.'

'Why?'

Bile rose into her throat. Swallowing it down she said, 'That has nothing to do with this.'

A hooded gaze still fixed to her face, he said, 'Why did you ask your solicitor if Cathy had any rights to your great-aunt's estate?'

Driven into a corner, Sanchia hesitated before admitting, 'I thought she might try to contest the will.'

Caid examined her with a chilling, impersonal interest, his handsome face a mask. 'So you don't trust her.'

Sanchia jumped to her feet and paced across the room, her hair flying about her clammy face as she shook her head and demanded, 'What is this, a cross-examination?'

He shrugged, but the hard blue gaze kept her pinned. 'Do you think she's capable of deception?'

The cool, merciless inquisition and the formality of his language made him seem distant, an alien, not the man who had kissed her so hungrily. Sanchia said wearily, 'Deception— yes, I suppose so, but this is forgery you're talking about! And fraud!'

He looked back at the document. 'Whatever the truth, I'll get to the bottom of it.'

His gaze lifted, catching her unawares. Three long strides brought him to stand in front of her. 'And perhaps you'd like to tell me why the mention of Cathy Tregear drains all the colour from your skin and steals the light from your eyes.'

A note in his voice sent tiny chills across her nerves. 'You're imagining things.'

Caid smoothed a tress of silky black hair away from her damp cheek. Was she telling the truth, or ruthlessly sacrificing an aunt she clearly had reason to dislike? His glance shifted to the pulse in her long throat, beating hard and heavily, and a fierce satisfaction rushed through him. She wore some faint perfume glossed with the scent of the sea, heady and altogether too potent. A primitive lust stirred.

And then he met her eyes—all emotions hidden by flat, opaque green enamel. Was she a bloody clever little actress and that fiery passion a fraud, or was she telling the truth?

Did the mysterious Cathy hold the key to Sanchia's reluctant response to him, to the panic that flared in her whenever he touched her?

Before he started applying real pressure he'd have to dig a lot deeper.

'Why should that surprise you?' she asked jaggedly. 'People often don't get on, and I wasn't an easy child to have around after my parents died—I was sulky and traumatised and desperate. Cathy was much younger than my mother, and she didn't want a twelve-year-old giraffe in her life.'

There was more to it than that, Caid realised. For a taut second she'd looked terrified—

the kind of sick, hopeless terror that you saw in kids caught up in the obscenity of war. And she wasn't twisting away from him as she would normally; she didn't even seem to realise that he was touching her at all. A fierce, bewildering protectiveness wrenched him.

The fine black strands of her hair slid cleanly across his skin, cool as running water, still damp from the sea, hair like the sultry promise of a tropical midnight. What would it be like to lie on a bed surrounded by that hair, see her great eyes glaze with passion as those long legs gripped his thighs in the most intimate embrace of all? What would it feel like to sate himself with that slim, silken body? Perhaps, he thought with an attempt at cynicism, he wanted her so much because she was the one who'd got away.

Tough common sense reined in his hardening body. Not yet. Not until he knew why she dissolved into flames in his arms, only to reject him a few seconds later. It could, of course, be a ploy to keep him off balance and stop him thinking too hard about the money he'd lost.

It took all his control to say indolently, 'I imagine that you were a quiet, well-behaved little girl, eager to love and be loved.'

When she flinched every instinct went onto red alert. Releasing the satiny tress he said, 'Sorry, did I pull it?'

'No.' The word cracked, her natural huskiness emphasised to near-hoarseness. Muscles moved jerkily in her pale throat as she swallowed.

Because he'd touched her hair? His gut tightened as he recalled how astonishingly responsive she was to him, but his instinct, always good, told him she wasn't reacting to him now.

Calmly, deliberately, he asked, 'So you don't know where Catherine Tregear is?'

The answer came too quickly. 'No.' Her fingers twined over and under until she'd knotted them together.

Caid strode across the room to stare out at the shimmering garden, limp and golden under the relentless sun, buzzing with bees and insects, while he fought a silent battle with himself.

Never before had he let his healthy male libido tangle his brain. It didn't seem likely, but if Sanchia was using her smoky eyes and silken skin and exquisite racehorse limbs to cheat him, she'd be dealt with the same way as everyone else who'd headed down that un-profitable path. Without mercy.

And when she'd learned her lesson he'd see that she never forgot it.

He'd also, he decided grimly, find out what trauma in her past imprisoned her. Something, he'd swear, to do with Cathy Tregear.

Sanchia watched him from beneath lowered lashes, wondering at the tension that pulsed through his big, graceful body. She had to clear her throat and suck breath back into her lungs before she could walk over to the table with the faxed sheets on it and gaze down at the signature.

Caid's voice made her jump. 'Do you have an address for Catherine Tregear?' When Sanchia hesitated he said drily, 'I can find it in the telephone directory.'

He'd do just that. Reluctantly she said, 'In my address book. I'll get it from the bach when I can go back.'

'Thank you.'

She no longer took his indifference at face value. He was going to track Cathy down. She said tautly, 'I hope the fire brigade gets here soon. Oh, we should have told them—the engine won't be able to get down the hill.'

'I imagine they'll use the smaller engine.'

'I didn't know they had two.'

He shrugged. 'A couple of years ago they had a big fund-raising drive for a new one.'

No doubt he'd contributed largely. Although no amounts had ever been mentioned, the mysterious transference of information in the district meant that everyone knew he was a generous donor to local causes.

Sanchia glowered down at her green shift, noting a grass stain on one side. Banning the memories that ambushed her—the scent of the grass, the heat and leonine strength of his big body, and the panic that had followed her first leaping, fiery response—she said again, 'I hope they get here soon.'

'Well, the bach isn't going to explode right now,' the fire chief said, her shrewd gaze moving from Sanchia's face to Caid's, 'but I certainly wouldn't say it's safe.'

When the volunteer brigade had arrived Caid had wanted Sanchia to wait at his house, but she'd insisted on going down with him.

He must have seen that he'd have to carry out his threat to tie her to a tree if he wanted to keep her away because he'd conceded, 'You can come if you do exactly as they say.'

She looked at him. 'I didn't ask you for permission,' she said sweetly, 'and of course I'll do what they say. I'm not stupid.'

Unexpectedly he gave her a slow, spectacular smile. 'No, merely stroppy and headstrong,' he said wryly. 'All right, let's go.'

'The gas bottle is faulty,' the fire chief told them now. 'It looks as though someone's taken to the connection with a heavy implement, perhaps trying to steal it.'

'Who'd do that?' Sanchia asked, feeling sick.

Caid said shortly, 'There have been incidents—people coming down to party on the beach. Terry, Will and Pat chased them away.'

Giving Sanchia a deeply envious glance, the fire chief said, 'Whatever, it's not safe. As well as the dodgy gas bottle, the electrical system is completely shot.' She pointed out a socket that had wobbled and sparked for as long as Sanchia remembered. 'That's highly dangerous, and it's not the only one. I've turned the power off; don't turn it back on.'

'It's all right to go inside?' Caid asked.

'The place probably won't explode,' the older woman repeated, 'but it's a fire waiting to happen.'

'I'll help you get your clothes,' Caid said to Sanchia. 'You can stay with us.'

Sanchia walked in through the open doors. A faint scent of gas still lingered on the hot air. Stepping carefully through the crumbling remains of the happiest years of her life, she led the way into her bedroom.

'What else do you want?' Caid asked. 'Photographs? Keepsakes?'

She stared around. 'No, I've taken all those. I'll collect the mugs—oh, the car.' She swung around, just preventing herself from colliding with him. 'I have to get the car away.'

'We'll put everything in it and take it up to the house.' Caid opened the wardrobe and began to scoop clothes from hangers with a ruthless efficiency that didn't rob his actions of a false intimacy.

The only way to stop him was to do it herself, so Sanchia emptied the drawers and rescued her toiletries from the bathroom and the food from the kitchen. Also from the kitchen she collected salt and pepper shakers in the shape of perky pigs, so old the glaze had cracked, and Great-Aunt Kate's mug, with the pukeko striding flamboyantly past a flax bush, and the matching teapot.

Once everything had been deposited in the car, Caid held out his hand. 'The keys.'

Sanchia said, 'I'll drive.'

The fire chief opened her mouth, but before she could speak Caid said, 'We'll push it well away from the house before I start it.'

Sanchia dithered, scanning his angular face, hard, totally determined; he wasn't going to give in.

'Good idea,' the fire chief seconded, and yelled for some strong arms from her crew.

Testosterone, Sanchia decided irritably, bending down to help push the car, had a lot to answer for.

It didn't take long to heave the small vehicle to a safe distance from the house. The fire crew stood at the ready while Caid got in and turned the key. Sanchia's breath blocked her throat until the engine caught, the car gave its usual little shudder, and the bach remained intact.

Sanchia wiped a suddenly shaky hand across her wet brow and walked swiftly towards the vehicle. Caid got out, holding the door open for her as she slid in behind the wheel. 'Thank you,' she said from the car to both Caid and the fire chief. 'I'm very grateful.'

It was the woman who answered. 'No problem. Take care.'

'I will.'

Caid walked around to the passenger's seat, all long legs and broad shoulders and masculine presence. When the door closed Sanchia put the car in gear and drove across the grassy paddock and up the steep hillside beneath the kanuka scrub and tree ferns.

Halfway back to his house, Caid said in an amused voice, 'Stop sulking.'

'I'm not sulking.' She skewered him with a pointed glance before switching her attention back to the road. 'I'm working out what I should do next.'

'Ring your insurance agent and the solicitor,' he told her promptly. 'You need to know where you stand with the insurance, and as the will hasn't been probated you should tell Jameson about the bach.'

Tightening her lips, she negotiated a pothole. 'I'd already realised that, but Mr Jameson is in the South Island walking the Heaphy Track so it will have to wait until he gets back. I'd better let my flatmates know I'm on my way back to Auckland.'

'It would be more convenient if you remained here until you've organised everything. There are plenty of spare bedrooms in the house and both my mother and I would enjoy your company.'

Her hands clenched onto the steering wheel; hoping he hadn't noticed, she straightened the car. Colour burned her cheeks as she said evenly, 'Thank you for offering—'

'A bedroom and a few meals,' he said in a bored voice. 'No big deal, Sanchia.'

Perhaps not for him, but it was turning into one for her. With this runaway sensual awareness firing her hormones into overdrive, accepting his hospitality could well be an act of foolhardy recklessness.

Nevertheless, he was right. She needed to stay close by because she'd arranged to meet a representative from the District Council in two days' time. 'I'll stay tonight,' she said, 'and find a motel tomorrow.'

'You'll be lucky.'

Right again; slap in the middle of the holiday season, every motel and bed and breakfast would be booked out. In silence she parked by the house, thinking wryly that her car was probably the oldest, tattiest vehicle ever to insult the gravel forecourt.

The sun heated blue flames in his hair as Caid got out. 'It's like driving a sardine tin. How do you manage to fit those long legs behind the wheel?'

Sanchia gave him a cool smile. 'We peasants get used to such inconveniences.' She parried his narrowed glance with fortitude.

Smoothly he said, 'Anyone less like a peasant it would be hard to imagine.' His gaze burned the length of her throat, settled for a searing milli-second on the thrust of her small, high breasts.

Hot, angry with him, but more with herself for offering him the opportunity and then responding with such pagan vehemence to his insolent survey, she said huskily, 'Thank you, I think.'

He picked up her suitcase and strode ahead into the quiet house. 'Try this for size,' he said, pushing open a door into a room. 'It looks over the Bay, so you'll be able to keep an eye on the bach through the trees.'

The room was large and light, its furniture luxurious yet with a stylishly casual air that fitted well into the relaxed ambience. Decorated in warm shades of cream and subtle dusky apricots and golds, it was the most opulent bedroom Sanchia had ever been in.

'There's a bathroom through there,' he told her, nodding at a door in the wall. 'If you need anything give Terry a call.'

Terry—housekeeper, dedicated cook and Caid's employee—was an old friend of Sanchia's.

Waiting until he'd closed the door behind him, she sat in a comfortable chair, pulled a card from her wallet, and rang through to the company that dealt with her aunt's insurance.

Ten minutes later she walked out of the room.

Caid must have been listening for her, because before she'd taken three steps he appeared at his office door. He frowned when he saw her face. 'Trouble?'

She said wearily, 'Robots passed me on to Whangarei and then to Auckland, I think, although it might have been Head Office in Timbuktu or Outer Mongolia. Whatever, no one is going to communicate. I left a message in someone's voicemail, and I owe you for the call.'

'You owe me nothing,' he said arrogantly.

A low, distant thunder abruptly changed position to erupt a few feet above the house. Sanchia blinked. 'What on earth—?'

'A helicopter—my mother must have arrived a day early,' he told her, black brows meeting across his arrogant nose in a frown that was immediately banished. The noise of the chopper died away to a slow thump, thump, thump as it landed. He smiled at her, brilliant eyes half concealed by heavy lids, his expression so bland she distrusted it immediately. 'Come on, we'll meet her.'

Going out with him seemed to imply some sort of intimacy. 'You'll want to be alone.'

'Just her, me and the chopper pilot?' he asked sardonically. 'With Terry and Will probably in hot pursuit?'

Foiled, she was reduced to muttering, 'You know what I mean.'

He touched her shoulder, a light fingertip contact that burned right through her. 'Stop making problems where none exist. Come on.'

Wordlessly she went with him, shading her eyes with her hand as they walked across the forecourt and into the paddock next door, its concrete pad now graced by a fussy white and red helicopter. No hot, summer-busy roads for the Hunters!

His mother, a trim, short woman with black hair and superb taste in clothes, was already on the ground, supervising the unloading of several large suitcases.

When Caid called out something in Greek she swivelled around, her face lighting up. Although, Sanchia noted with a jolt of dismay, she cast an extremely sharp glance Sanchia's way before hurling herself open-armed at her son.

After they'd embraced she disentangled herself quickly, saying ebulliently, 'It *is* Sanchia, isn't it? Little Sanchia Smith? I knew it—I'd recognise those legs anywhere, and that glorious hair. And your lovely face, my dear. I was so sad to hear of your great-aunt's death, but she had such a wonderful life, with you to brighten it for her final years. Now *smile* at me!'

And when Sanchia broke into surprised laughter, the older woman nodded with satisfaction. 'Yes, that wonderful, wonderful smile. I remember how difficult it was to coax from you!'

Caid said, 'Mama, I'm trying to persuade Sanchia to stay with us for a few days. The bach has a gas leak and a very dangerous electrical system, as well as an empty water tank.'

Sending an indignant glance at him, Sanchia said, 'But I can't just—'

'Just what?' Mrs Hunter's dark eyes opened wide. 'Of course you must stay—this is a big house and I won't bother you, not a bit. I come here each year to rest, to recuperate—ask Caid. He'll tell you I just lie around and recharge my batteries and practise being a grandmother in my mind.'

Caid flung his head back and laughed while Sanchia said hastily, 'Oh, that's not—I mean, of course you won't bother me! I just don't want to be a nuisance.'

'You won't be a nuisance.' A small hand fastened onto her arm. With more than a hint of her son's determination, Mrs Hunter swept her into the house, leaving Caid and the pilot and Will Spence—Terry's husband, who'd emerged from the garden—to bring in the luggage.

'It sounds like a chapter of disasters,' Mrs Hunter said sympathetically, heading for the terrace. 'Come, let us sit down and you can tell me all about it.'

It was going to be difficult to keep saying no to Mrs Hunter. And surely with Mrs Hunter in residence she'd be safe from this unsettling, primitive urge to forget everything about common sense and self-protection and the secret that made it impossible for her to ever give in to Caid's intense, sexual charisma.

Her mood a mixture of chagrin and reluctant, guilty anticipation, Sanchia sat down opposite Mrs Hunter in the shade of a jasmine vine.

The older woman regarded her benignly. 'Now, tell me exactly what has happened.'

Mrs Hunter responded to Sanchia's explanation with gentle clucks that soothed some raw patch she hadn't even known her psyche possessed. Although her parents had loved her they'd never been demonstrative, and Great-Aunt Kate had been brisk and unsentimental.

'Caid smelt gas, and he—' She swallowed, conscious again of how dangerous that drifting gas could have been. Steadying her voice, she finished on a valiant half-laugh, 'He almost *threw* me out of the house and behind the tank and rolled on top to protect me.'

'He's always had very fast reactions, very keen senses,' his mother said, possessing herself of Sanchia's hand and patting it. 'What a shock, my poor girl! Of course you must stay here for as long as you're in Northland.'

Tears clogged Sanchia's throat. She didn't know what to do with her hand; it seemed rude to drag it away, so she left her fingers in Mrs Hunter's clasp, hauled a handkerchief from her pocket with her spare hand and blew her nose.

Apparently considering this a perfectly normal way to deal with the situation, Mrs Hunter made more soothing comments until the tightness in Sanchia's throat had relaxed and she was able to say gruffly, 'You're very kind.'

'Not at all. What will you do about the bach?'

'If I can ever speak to someone at the insurance company instead of disembodied voices, I might be able to find out,' Sanchia said bitterly.

'Caid will hurry them up,' Mrs Hunter said with complete conviction in her son's ability to move mountains.

Caid emerged from the house, overshadowing the magnificent seascape so completely that Sanchia decided his mother was probably right. Moving mountains no doubt rated high on his list of accomplishments.

After a quick glance at Sanchia he began to talk easily of his mother's trip from New York; Sanchia settled back into her chair, tucking her legs under it as she listened to their undemanding conversation.

Within a few minutes Terry appeared with tea; when they'd drunk it Caid looked across at Sanchia and said pleasantly, 'Could you give me that address now?'

Although couched as a request, there was no doubt it was a command. Sanchia stared at him in bewilderment.

'Your aunt's—Catherine Tregear,' he reminded her.

Even then she could only think of Great-Aunt Kate, until she remembered Cathy. Mortified, she got to her feet. 'Yes, of course,' she said colourlessly, and smiled at Mrs Hunter before walking along the wide, sunny hall to her bedroom.

It took a moment or two of fossicking in her bag to find the tiny book. As her fingers closed on it the hair stirred on the back of her neck and she swung around. Silent as a panther, Caid had followed her to the door. Her heart beating high in her throat, Sanchia read out the address.

'Can you write it down for me?' he asked.

She wrote it out, tore the page from her notebook and handed it over.

He glanced at it. 'You have pretty writing.'

What an odd thing to say. And what a weird response from her—a kind of primal, bone-deep shudder as his finger skimmed over the page. 'Thank you.'

In a way, she thought, striving to be objective, his stunning good looks were a snare; at first impression Caid Hunter was the modern equivalent of a young Greek god, but a second glance revealed that the classical features, the dramatic colouring, the heart-shaking glamour of Caid's face were based on a tough, implacable framework. In spite of his magnetic sexuality, he bore himself like a ruler.

No one would ever doubt that in the often vicious cut and thrust of the business world Caid Hunter wielded enormous power. It wasn't just his clothes that proclaimed it, although they bore the stamp of an extremely good tailor. Nor was it the thin gold watch, or the inborn confidence often possessed by the offspring of the very rich; simply, Caid was a man who faced the world on his own terms, a man accustomed to winning.

He folded the scrap of paper and stowed it into his pocket. 'Why don't you try to forget about everything but enjoying your holiday?'

It was an order, not a suggestion. 'As soon as I've tracked down a human being at the insurance company I will,' she said, and wondered why she'd lied.

Enjoyable was the last way to describe this edgy, potent, ambiguous relationship. If she wasn't extremely careful, Sanchia thought, watching him walk out of the room, she might even fancy herself in love with him again.

And that would be a total disaster, just as it had been three years ago.

CHAPTER SIX

'I WONDERED,' Caid said casually over dinner on the terrace, 'if you'd like to come with me tomorrow.'

Sanchia's stomach clenched. 'I—where are you going?'

'To check out a property development.' His enigmatic eyes met her wary glance.

To hide the weakness that urged her to agree, she asked crisply, 'Don't you delegate that sort of supervision to underlings?'

His brows lifted, but he said mildly enough, 'This one is special.'

No doubt he wanted to show her how *special* any development of Waiora Bay would be. Sanchia's fork stayed poised over her plate. 'But Hunter's is famous for its prize-winning, ecologically stringent, exclusive developments.' Damn, did that sound as though she spent her spare time searching newspapers and magazines for information about him? 'Your mother—' she said, too swiftly to be polite.

He interrupted, 'My mother usually needs a day to recover from jet lag. I'm sure she'd like tomorrow to herself in a quiet house.'

Mrs Hunter had retired early after announcing that her body clock needed silence and a tray in her room and a good night's sleep to get itself into sync with New Zealand time.

Forking up a delectable piece of lamb, Sanchia said, 'You don't have to entertain me, Caid.'

'I'd rather hoped you might entertain me,' he told her outrageously. A challenge glinted in his heavy-lidded eyes, in the mocking, beautiful curve of his lips—a challenge he probably expected her to refuse with righteous indignation.

'Entertaining men is not my strong point, but I'll come with you,' she said perversely, and ate the lamb. Served as an entrée with voluptuous purple and cream eggplant slices and the sharp white and green of a minted yoghurt sauce, it had the same effect on her tastebuds as Caid's smile did on her spine. Meltdown.

Half closing her eyes to shut him out, Sanchia concentrated on her plate. When her employers were in residence the caretaker's wife, an inventive and dedicated cook, relished the opportunity to show off her skills.

'Good, I'll be leaving about ten.'

A raw note in his voice snagged her attention. He was watching her with a deliberately blank face, but leashed emotions smouldered in his eyes.

Swallowing hastily, Sanchia banished a treacherous, wildfire surge of satisfaction. 'I'll be ready.' Because her mind refused to function beyond the most basic inanities, she added, 'Terry's outdone herself with this meal. I'll bet she's been practising on Will.'

'He looks remarkably fit on it.' Caid's eyes were now limpid and unreadable and his voice revealed nothing but cool, ironic amusement.

Years ago, at a friend's birthday party, Sanchia had watched a film on television, a vintage swashbuckler where the hero and villain had fought a duel. As their swords clashed in the light of the rising sun the actors had managed to convey deadly artistry combined with a powerful masculine exhilaration at facing a worthy opponent.

Sanchia felt like that now—determined, rash, defiant—and alight with a glinting excitement. An excitement she couldn't indulge because it would lead to inevitable humiliation, she thought, lifting her square chin and changing the subject. 'This is a superb setting for dinner.'

Although the sun was low in the western sky, its heat had driven them to eat beneath a creeper-draped pergola. The jasmine's clustered buds and white, sweetly scented flowers starred the glossy foliage that twined above and around them.

Sanchia tried to blame the drifting, provocative perfume for this consuming, mysterious awareness, this feeling of being exposed and defenceless. Caid didn't seem affected by it, or by the soft hush of the waves on the beach below, or the drowsy warmth of the evening as it slid lazily, imperceptibly into a summer night.

'My mother is an incurable romantic.' Caid's wry words didn't hide his affection. 'She creates settings wherever she goes; this is one of her favourites.'

Sanchia forced her failing brain into action. 'She obviously makes the trends. When this house was built nobody thought the

Mediterranean look would be the next big thing.'

'The Mediterranean look is in her blood. She grew up on a small island off Corfu and she carries it in her heart wherever she goes.'

Sanchia nodded. 'Yes,' she said simply.

'Is that why you don't want to sell, even though you can't live here? Because the Bay is the home of your heart?'

Such acute perception iced through her. Not for the first time she recognised the wrench it would be to give up Waiora Bay. 'I—yes.'

'Where did you live with your parents?'

A sip of delicious, tangy Sauvignon Blanc gave her a moment to collect her thoughts. She swallowed the wine and said huskily, 'On their yacht—the *Seabird*.'

Caid matched her movement, watching her over the rim as he drank for intimate, disturbingly erotic seconds. Shock waves shivered down her spine to pool in surging disarray in the pit of her stomach.

Fixing her eyes on the pale golden liquid in her glass, she hurried on, 'We travelled all around the Pacific. My father couldn't live on land—he was a wanderer.'

'How did he earn a living?'

'He wrote articles for magazines and news-papers.' She let another small mouthful of wine trickle down her throat. 'And three or four books. Occasionally someone tells me that his books and articles fed their dream of sailing to tropical islands. Most of them knew they'd never get there, so he lived the dream for them.'

'An interesting childhood,' Caid observed, that keen gaze never leaving her face. 'Did you go to school?'

'Whenever we stayed anywhere for more than a week.' She set her glass down. 'Travelling gave me a grounding in languages—you learn to communicate really fast when you're starved of company. At sea my parents taught me.'

His mouth curved. 'I'll bet you wanted to live in a house.'

Sanchia gave him a startled look. 'How did you guess?'

'Seems to be the way kids think. We went back to my mother's family in Greece at least once a year, calling in at London or Rome or somewhere exotic on the way to or from. Yet all I ever wanted was a bach at the beach like the ones my friends went to every summer.' He turned his dark head and looked through the swooping branches of the pohutukawa trees. 'Like your great-aunt's. I was so excited when my father bought this place. When I saw the house I was disgusted because it was just the same as our other houses!' His mouth curved as Sanchia laughed, then he said idly, 'Your great-aunt told me that your parents died at sea.'

'Yes. In a cyclone off Australia.' Her voice was steady, almost off-hand. 'A helicopter arrived but they only had time and fuel for one pass overhead.'

He frowned. 'What stopped them winching up your parents with you?'

'My mother wouldn't leave my father; he was trapped in the wreckage of the mast and the rigging.' Sanchia looked down at her plate. 'He'd broken his back, I think, and we couldn't cut him free.'

His mouth compressed. 'I see.'

Did he? 'They were a devoted couple. I'm glad they went together—I don't think my mother would have survived without him. She worshipped him.'

'So she abandoned you.'

The note of harsh condemnation in his voice brought a swift response. 'It's a decision no human being should ever have to make.'

'I agree.' He turned the glass in his hand so that the candles gleamed in small, scintillating flashes in the wine. Deliberately, almost brutally, he said, 'Yet you were still a child, and a very vulnerable one. Your mother must have known what her sister was like—the sort of life she led.'

He had voiced her hidden, mute resentment, displayed it for her to face in all its ugliness.

Sanchia said quietly, 'Decisions made after thirty sleepless, terrifying hours at the mercy of a cyclone aren't always sensible. My father was still conscious; she couldn't leave him to die alone.'

'Not even when he knew you'd be living with a woman I wouldn't entrust with the care of a termite? He should have forced your mother to leave him,' he said curtly.

Caid would have, Sanchia realised, nerves tensing as she took in his hard, dominating features; he had enormous strength of will. But it wasn't this realisation that lifted the hairs on the back of her neck. Shaping the words carefully she asked, 'How do you know so much about Cathy?'

His broad shoulders lifted. 'I've just received a preliminary report about her. It makes interesting reading; she's notorious in her own small way, your aunt.' When she swallowed he added coolly, 'If I accept that you and Kate Tregear had nothing to do with forging that annuity agreement, then Cathy is the only other logical suspect.'

'I—yes, I know.'

He said calmly, 'Did you know she was married?'

Sanchia looked up. 'No!'

His face was pitiless, a mask of gold in the last rays of the sun. 'To a Robert Atkins, I believe.'

Panic beat wildly through Sanchia; dimly she heard her fork hit the table with a soft clunk. Then the low hum of wheels and Terry's voice instructing her husband to be careful broke into the drumming silence. A moment later the Spences emerged from the house with a trolley.

Only once before in her life had Sanchia been so pleased to be interrupted.

'How was that?' Terry asked, efficiently removing the empty plates.

'Fishing for compliments?' Caid asked with a smile.

Terry grinned at him. 'A woman needs to be appreciated,' she said, 'and a cook even more so.'

'It was delicious, as ever. Thank you.'

Sanchia said, 'On a scale of ten it probably ranks around fifteen.' Her voice sounded a little higher than normal, but not enough to be marked.

Terry beamed. 'Just wait until you've tasted this!'

'Something new?' Caid's brows rose. 'How many times did she make you try it, Will?'

'Five,' the caretaker said dismally, helping Terry unload dishes. He went on, 'Though I didn't mind—it's good.'

Salmon fillets glowed rosily over scallops that had been sautéed in a nutty oil, and Terry had chosen to match the seafood with a pasta that combined—against all odds—Italian and Asian flavours in a glorious homage to both. All appetite fled, Sanchia wondered how she was going to control the churning in her stomach enough to force down a couple of mouthfuls.

'Enjoy,' Terry bade them as she and Will disappeared back into the house.

'She's a wonderful cook,' Sanchia said, taking crisp lettuce from a bowl as she tried to control her jumping nerves.

'Superb.'

Was he going to return to the subject of Cathy? Not if she could prevent it! 'And you take it entirely for granted.'

Caid drawled, 'What do I take for granted?'

His tone was a warning, but she wasn't going to back down. 'Brilliant staff, and this house—only a holiday house to you, but much grander than normal people ever aspire to— and the helicopter to ferry you around above the clogged roads. All the ways the very rich insulate themselves from the rest of us.'

'Go on,' he said silkily when she stopped.

Sanchia took a deep breath; might as well be hung for a sheep... 'Even the hundred and twenty thousand dollars you say you've been cheated of can't be more than a financial irritation. I suspect that what really galls you is being outwitted.'

Easily, almost conversationally, he said, 'You'd better believe it, Sanchia. And also believe that I'm going to pursue whoever defrauded me until I'm satisfied that the perpetrator has paid—fully.'

Cold foreboding settled between her shoulders and scudded down her spine.

He lifted his glass again in a taunting salute. 'I've worked for everything I've got, and so did my father. My mother, too. She ran the office in the early years and held off having children until the business was solvent. When he died she sold everything—her jewels, their art collection, every house but this place—to keep the business solvent. She'd have sold this too if I hadn't stopped her.'

'I didn't know that,' Sanchia said in a muted voice.

'Of course luck has played a part in Hunter's success, but it's been luck underpinned by bloody hard work. That's why I don't consider a hundred and twenty thousand

dollars a small deal.' He glanced towards the
house. 'It represents a lot of sacrifices made by
my mother. And I despise thieves; I've worked
too hard to feel anything but contempt for
someone who wants to steal from me.'

'Yes,' Sanchia said quietly. 'I can understand that.'

He settled back in his chair, his smile a dangerous mixture of enjoyment and mockery.
'How did a Puritan come to have a mouth like
yours?' he murmured. 'Soft and red and passionate—all promises and innocent provocation—yet held under ferocious restraint. Have
you ever been tempted to ease up on that control, Sanchia?'

His voice had been designed for seduction,
she thought confusedly, deep and steady and
deceptively smooth with a fascinating abra-
siveness just below the surface; when he
turned his wicked, unsparing charm onto her
she longed to surrender.

A surrender that would end in terror and humiliation.

Attack, she thought, leaning forward. 'Did
you have to take lessons in seduction,' she

asked sweetly, 'or were you born knowing how to do it?'

He bent across the table until his face was a mere six inches or so away. Caution urged a retreat, yet Sanchia refused stubbornly to move. Bold blue buccaneer's eyes imprisoned hers; in them she read a determination that set alarm sirens shrieking.

'Your beautiful mouth is a bit too smart,' he said quietly, and kissed her.

She tried to shake her head, but it was too late; the moment his mouth claimed hers a ferocious blast of desire overruled her last pleading remnant of common sense.

Demanding, confident, his kiss stole everything from her, rendered her witless and without will-power under the lash of need.

When he pulled back she made a soft sound that registered dismay even as she strove to subdue her violent, clamorous hunger.

'Yes,' he agreed, his voice uneven, a lean hand splaying on the table as he got to his feet and came around the table in a noiseless rush.

He pulled her upright and into his arms. Still dazed, Sanchia stared into a face honed by consuming need.

While she drowned in his smile, he bent his black head and kissed her again, on her mouth, and then her eyelids, and when she lifted her head in mute entreaty his knowledgeable lips found the tender line of her jaw and the sensitive length of her white throat.

Dazzled by deep-seated emotions that scared her more than the unleashed sensuality raging through her bloodstream, Sanchia knew that never again would she be able to smell the scent of jasmine without remembering this moment.

For a second—a fraction of a heartbeat—she relaxed in his arms, hoping that at last she was free of the terror.

Only to feel it surge like a hideous beast in her unconscious. With a low, anguished cry she began to struggle.

Immediately she was free. Her breath blocked her throat; swaying, she put out a hand and supported herself on the table. Beneath her acutely sensitised fingertips the texture of the fine linen cloth felt rough, abrasive.

Eyes guarded, his face set in dangerous, unsmiling lines, Caid said, 'I keep trying to find out when your mouth will deliver on the promises it makes. One of these days you might trust me enough to tell me why it doesn't.'

'No,' she said heavily, stiffening her spine.

'Why, Sanchia?' His voice was almost gentle.

Staring down at the wavering lights of the candles, dancing like witchlights in the rapidly thickening dusk, she said woodenly, 'Because there's nothing to tell you.'

Because if she did, he'd feel sorry for her, and pity was the one emotion she didn't want from him.

There was a moment's silence, during which she kept her gaze fixed on the cutlery.

Steel reinforced his words as Caid said, 'Or nothing you can bear to tell me?'

Desperately, her brain racing, she muttered, 'Caid, I know there's—something between—'

'You know I want you,' he interrupted with brutal honesty.

'Why? I've seen photographs of the women you take out. I know there's a huge gulf between them and me,' she retorted, pride bringing her head up. 'A man who finds Leila Sherif attractive isn't going to look at me unless he has an ulterior motive.'

With eyes as piercing as the kiss of a sword-blade, he said, 'I don't know what blind idiot made you feel inferior—perhaps the same one who made you so terrified of your own sexuality—but I give you fair warning: I want you, and that has nothing to do with anyone's plans for the Bay.'

While she stared at him he smiled again and touched the pulse that beat wildly in her throat. 'And you want me,' he said softly before he took a step back. 'Even though anything beyond a kiss frightens the hell out of you. One day you'll tell me why.'

Never. Fighting for control, Sanchia managed to produce a sketchy shrug. Sickening remnants of panic churned through her, scrambling her brain, tormenting her with glimpses of things that might have been if only she hadn't gone to live with Cathy—if only...

What poet had said that *if only* were the two saddest words in the language?

Sanchia angled her chin and sat down again, staring at Terry's delectable meal as though it was salvation. 'I find you very attractive,' she said as calmly as she could, clamping down on the aching need, the yearning that had never left her. 'But I realised three years ago that apart from that attraction we have nothing in common. I didn't want an affair then; I haven't changed my mind.'

He stood a few feet away, a shadow on the rapidly darkening terrace. The small lights of the candles flickered, warming the sculpted lines of his face, burnishing the dark skin into glowing bronze. He looked like a barbarian warrior, a man of iron and blood, as he demanded, 'Is that why you ran away? Because you thought we had nothing in common?'

'Yes,' she said, and it was only half a lie. Refusing to look at him, she pushed a piece of salmon under the pasta, then dropped the fork onto her plate because her hand trembled so much. The tiny tinkle of sound counterpointed the slow hush of the waves.

'Perhaps,' Caid asked with ruthless, exquisite courtesy, 'you could explain a little further.'

She sensed disbelief in his tone, his stance, a hand in one pocket, rocking back on his heels as he looked at her. She said curtly, 'You know exactly what I mean. I didn't then—and I don't now—feel like playing Cinderella to your Prince Charming. Especially as I'd be demoted to scullery maid again when it was all over.'

'I've always thought the interesting thing about that story is that the prince didn't care whether she was a scullery maid.' The words bit into the soft, warm air. 'He insisted that every woman in the kingdom try on the abandoned shoe.'

She'd never thought of this before, and couldn't afford to consider it now. 'I didn't break your heart three years ago, Caid. A month later you were burning up all the gossip columns with that stunning model, Florencia someone.'

The moment the words left her mouth she knew she'd give anything to recall them, but it was too late.

She saw a flash of white in the darkness as he smiled. The dark aura of danger faded slightly as he came back to the table and sat down. Still smiling, he said calmly, 'Just Florencia on its own. Eat up. You're staring at Terry's wonderful—and much appreciated—' he emphasised drily '—food as though it's a nest of scorpions. You can relax; you've made your attitude plain. I don't come on to women in my household, so you're safe in your cold little cocoon until this business with the house is dealt with.'

'Do you know how arrogant you sound? *My household!*'

He grinned. 'I'm half-Greek,' he told her, 'and it goes with the genes. Don't make the mistake of thinking I don't mean exactly what I say. I believe in honesty and openness, but I also believe that in nature man is the hunter and woman his natural prey—that he pursues her until she chooses him or refuses him.'

Although laughter glinted in his eyes as he scanned her outraged expression, he wasn't joking. 'I do accept equality of the sexes, however—so if *you* want to pursue *me* I promise I won't feel harassed,' he finished with an ironic tilt of his head.

'Being half-Greek,' she said, shaken yet valiant, 'is no excuse for strutting.'

His handsome, compelling face broke up into laughter.

Somehow he'd blindsided her. His frank avowal of pursuit had set every sense drumming turbulently, but his laughter soothed the panic his words—and his tone—had caused.

Before she could speak he said matter-of-factly, 'I hope you're not going to let your irritation with me stop you from considering my suggestion carefully.'

. She gave him a baffled look. 'What suggestion?'

'The one I'm about to make. Now that I know how much the Bay means to you, there's no reason why you should lose it entirely. We could come to some arrangement so you'd still have a home here. Not the bach, of course— that will have to be demolished.'

First the threats, now the sweetener, she thought sardonically. No matter what happened, the Bay was truly lost to her; Great-Aunt Kate had made it impossible for her to own it, and once she'd done what she had to do, she'd never go back.

Trying hard to be fair, she admitted silently that Caid wouldn't drive her away. Wrenched by a horrifying mixture of frustration and bitter grief, she said disjointedly, 'I won't accept anything from you—when I own a house it will be through my own efforts.'

'It still could be,' he said, watching her with an enigmatic interest that sent tiny shudders through her.

Colour burned up through her skin, fired her eyes, almost set her black hair ablaze. 'Not that way,' she said between her teeth.

The sun fell suddenly over the horizon and the waiting night pounced. Caid's smile was a masterpiece of irony. 'I don't know what you think I meant, but I certainly wasn't suggesting you sleep with me in payment. I don't need to buy sex, Sanchia. Eat up, or Terry will think you don't like her food.'

Silently, her appetite completely gone, Sanchia picked up her knife and fork. 'To coin a cliché, I'm not that sort of woman,' she said recklessly.

She was not any sort of woman—the thought of sex sickened her. The flake of salmon she ate tasted like flannel.

Caid sat gracefully down opposite her. 'I remember. No sordid affairs. Is there any man on the horizon?' His voice was insultingly casual.

A second stretched uncomfortably while she dithered. Eventually she returned, 'It's really none of your business.'

'As long as you respond to my kisses as passionately as you do, it's my business,' he drawled insolently.

Sanchia pushed some more fish around her plate. 'That's just physical attraction,' she said, glad that the rapid twilight hid her scorching cheeks. 'I'd have thought you were sophisticated enough to know that it means very little.'

'Oh, I know that. But do you?' As her mouth compressed he said blandly, 'Eat up, Sanchia. Perhaps we should keep to uncontroversial subjects for the rest of the evening. What do you think about the latest Booker Prize winner?'

The following day she stared along a dusty secondary road and said accusingly, 'This is the way to Macgregor's Bay.'

'Yes.'

'I came here once on a school outing and loved it.' Sanchia cleared her throat. Stupid to be disappointed; it made sense to develop the most exquisite beaches, and Caid was famous for his financial acumen. 'How many houses have been built there?'

'Five.'

Surprised, she asked, 'Surely there's room for a lot more than five?'

'Other developers had every intention of cutting it up into twenty sections,' he said levelly.

When Sanchia waited he went on, 'My development manager decided that the infrastructure wouldn't take it—the road's too narrow and widening it would cost a packet and be unsatisfactory.' He sent her a measured, inscrutable glance before fixing his gaze back onto the road. 'I agree. Five houses are enough.'

Ten minutes later Sanchia had to admit that the firm's architects had done a brilliant job. A semicircle of white sand on the southern edge of one of Northland's slender, twisting harbours, Macgregor's Bay was sheltered by a high, grassy headland from the winds and waves that pounded in from the Pacific.

The almost completed houses had been skilfully tucked between the access road and the beach, at a distance from one another yet close enough for a sense of community. Landscaping had begun, but the place was empty of people.

As she fell in beside Caid on the beach, he took a minuscule Dictaphone from his pocket and made sharp, pertinent comments into it. Safe behind the darkened lenses of her sunglasses, Sanchia watched. The man who'd been resolutely pleasant and uncontroversial since dinner last night became subtly transmuted; his face grew harder, more angular, and his voice rang with cool detachment and authority.

This, she thought, was the real Caid Hunter, the ruthless, unsparing autocrat who ruled a growing empire. And he hadn't acquired that empire by being nice to people.

Halfway along the beach he clicked the Dictaphone off. 'There's a covenant on the gardens. They have to be drought-proof.' He looked up at the dry, shaggy headland. 'When the autumn rains arrive that hill will be planted in native trees—the Department of Conservation has collected seeds from the few patches of local bush that are still left and grown them on.'

'They'll need care for some years.' The wild, salt-laden winds of winter and the arid heat of next summer would kill any untended plant.

'We've installed temporary irrigation. In two hundred years the headland might look a little as it did when the first Europeans came to New Zealand.'

'That would be wonderful,' she said.

'You sound startled.' Both words and tone goaded. 'Did you think we'd walk in here, blast everything flat and build apartment blocks along the beach?'

Bending, she tried to yank a twist of dry grass from her sandal. When it resisted she slipped off her sandal, balancing on one leg while she shook the straw out. Casually, Caid took the hand she held out for balance, supporting her with a warm, strong grip.

'Not exactly startled,' she said when the stem was free. She dropped the sandal and slid her foot back inside, pulling her hand away from his. Her voice wavered as she went on, 'You must admit that most developers only make a token gesture with a few palms and pohutukawas.'

'We are not ''most developers''.'

'I can see that. The houses look...'
Searching for the exact word, she hesitated,
then finished, 'They look right, fitting. And
they please the eye. Is this the sort of thing
you'd like to do at Waiora?'

'No,' he said, his perfectly pleasant voice
warning her off. 'Why do you dislike what's
been done here?'

And for once she'd tried for tact. 'I don't
dislike it. I'd just prefer it to be left undeveloped,' she said quietly. 'Which is stupid, because it's been farmed for over a hundred
years.'

'A bit naïve, certainly.' Still in that pleasant,
intimidating tone he went on, 'This place was
on the market. If we hadn't bought it and developed it someone else would have.'

'Yes, I know—'

'To keep coastal land undeveloped you need
to start working at District Council level to
change the system. As long as farmers are
forced to sell their land to pay the rates you'll
have development.'

She nodded. 'This is lovely—and it will be
even lovelier as the years go by.'

'Did it hurt to say that?'

'No,' she returned shortly.

His smile taunted her. 'If you can't put conviction into your tone you run the risk of being disbelieved.'

Exasperated, she said steadily, 'This will be a superb place for holidays. The houses have been built with discretion and that special ambience you get when both architect and designer are respectful of the landscape.'

'And you wouldn't live here if you were paid to.' Caid didn't know why he was pushing her.

Her green eyes smouldered and the full, passionate lips tightened. 'Don't put words into my mouth.'

Ignoring the flare of desire in his groin, he looked down at her. Something about her drove him wild—perhaps the contrast between her black cloud of hair and her skin, milky white and translucent, accented by those astonishing eyes and that sultry mouth. She walked like a dream—long-legged, lithe and graceful—and she challenged him on the most fundamental level. Cursing silently, he wondered what quixotic folly had persuaded him to give his word she'd be safe.

He could take her, he thought, trying to detach himself from a situation that was rapidly becoming dangerous. Something in Sanchia's eyes, in her husky, controlled voice, in the determined way she posted keep-off signs, told him she wouldn't reject him.

Not until the barriers came crashing up, and she stiffened and fought, unable to control her panic. Three years ago he'd thought her fear was because she was a virgin; she'd shattered his pride when she'd rejected him, and so he'd let her go when she ran.

Not now. If she wouldn't tell him what had happened, he'd have to find out. Her extreme reaction must indicate a terrifying sexual experience somewhere in her past. With the relentless anger he so rarely revealed, Caid decided that once he'd hunted down the man who'd ruined her inherent passion, he'd make him pay.

At least he knew she wasn't like so many other women, who looked at him and saw nice packaging backed up by dollars and sex.

It wasn't their fault that women had been programmed by nature to look for men who could give them security. Only a foolish man expected more—and yet his father, poor and proud, had met his mother, rich and indulged, on a simmering day in Greece and she'd given up everything, even her beloved family, to follow him half around the world. Her parents hadn't forgiven her until Caid had been born.

Was he suffering from a sudden rush of romanticism to the head for wanting the same sort of love from the woman he'd marry? Possibly it didn't even exist now; romance seemed out of fashion among his peers.

Nor would he find it with Sanchia. She might want him, but she didn't try to hide her dislike of everything he represented.

There was also the business of just who had extracted an annuity from him. His enquiries so far had revealed that Sanchia was right; her great-aunt had been christened Kate, and the signature on the papers was almost certainly a forgery.

What he hadn't discovered yet was who'd committed it. In spite of that damning initial report on Cathy Atkins, he couldn't yet discount the possibility that Sanchia's huge green eyes hid deceit. She wouldn't be the first woman who'd looked at him with eyes just as

smokily desirous as hers and lied through her
teeth.

He wouldn't let his testosterone make up his
mind for him.

Swinging on his heel, he said in a clipped
voice, 'I could build you something like this
at Waiora Bay.'

Sanchia could have hit him. Resisting the
impulse, she clenched her fists and sent a savage glance at the wide shoulders, the perfect
male triangle poised on lean hips and long,
muscular legs, and wished fervently that she
could knock him off that pinnacle of self-
confidence and watch him grovel.

Her low, furious voice emerged with hoarse
distinctness. 'I don't want anything from you.'

He swung around. Astonishingly he grinned,
although there was something disturbing and
sexy and challenging about it. 'One day,' he
said, 'I'll let you do exactly what you want to
do right now.'

'How do you know what I want to do?' she
asked icily. A reckless need to wring some
small surrender from him drove her to stalk
deliberately past, her hips swaying, her back
stiff. She'd never consciously tried to be pro-

vocative, but her body certainly knew how to go about it.

'Sanchia.'

The quiet, unyielding command stopped her in her tracks. Unwillingly she turned her head and looked at him. Half-closed, glittering eyes promised retribution, but he didn't move.

It wasn't enough. He knew, she thought confusedly, how to deal with simple, straightforward hunger, the primitive call of female to male. What she wanted was much deeper, more subtle, and yet more elemental than that; she wanted to smash through his cool, powerful defences and see him as naked and needy as she was.

She wanted to be as big a danger to him as he was to her. I'm falling in love with him again, she thought wildly. Oh, what the hell— I never fell *out* of love with him. These past three years have been a sham.

'Stop this,' he growled, all coiled aggression as he came up behind her.

'Stop what?'

'Stop trying to prod me into doing something I promised not to.' *Unless you want me to.*

The words of surrender hovered on her tongue, danced through her brain like the dare they'd been, almost made it to her vocal cords; she just managed to gulp them back, because although she wanted him with every wanton cell in her body, the thought of making love, of letting any man—even Caid—touch her and take her summoned all the demons, all the nightmares.

Ashamed, she said, 'I'm not responsible for your actions. I'm only responsible for my own.'

Although he smiled it didn't reach his eyes, and his tone showed no amusement. 'Then be responsible. You're being as provocative as you can be, inviting a response you don't really want.'

She said stolidly, 'If I ever proposition you, I'll put it in words you can't mistake.'

Laughing beneath his breath, he caught her shoulder. She stiffened, but relaxed as soon as she realised she'd misread him. Instead of the violence she feared, his fingers smoothed across her bare upper arm, skimming it gently, sliding under the green shell top to stroke the skin across her shoulder. Drowning in his brilliant blue gaze, she thought she could feel that light, persuasive touch through to the marrow of her bones, down to her toes.

Stop it right now, she commanded herself, eyes clinging to the arrogant sweep of his cheekbones, moving slowly up to meet his...

Sweat sprang out across her top lip, beaded her temples. The sun beat down on her head, burned into her arms, loosening her, weakening her. She could taste salt, and something else—the flavour of longing. That treacherous hunger summoned fire and frustration, a powerful yearning leashed only by fear.

His intent eyes, blue and deep as the finest sapphires, snared her, holding her as still as a rabbit caught in a car's headlights. The sun gilded the harsh, superb framework of his face, the perfect curves of his mouth. Yet he didn't tighten his grip, didn't move. Entranced by his prowling sensuality, she lifted a hand and traced the outline of his mouth, felt his humourless smile against her skin.

'How many lovers have you had?' he asked, his fingers curling around her shoulderblade, straying tormentingly to the sensitive nape of her neck.

The rough tracery of his fingertips over the satin slide of her skin sent more shivers racing the length of her spine. His faint male fragrance mingled with salt and newly mown grass to summon a turbulent sensuality from her, emphasised by the sibilant whisper of the waves, the harsh, demanding cry of a gull.

Caid bent his head. 'How many lovers?' he repeated. His breath fanned her lips. 'Have there been any, Sanchia?'

CHAPTER SEVEN

SANCHIA shook her head drowsily, then lifted a seeking face.

Caid dropped a swift, unsatisfying kiss onto her lips. 'Sweet Sanchia.' His voice was hypnotic, many-layered, at once soothing and charged with lazy sexuality. 'Sweet, fiery Sanchia,' he murmured, and kissed her again.

Only their mouths touched, clung, parted— met again. Sanchia's hands quivered, but some dim, wavering spark of common sense kept them clenched at her sides as the need that coiled deep inside her began to flow with silken insistence through every cell; it sharpened her senses to unbearable intensity and spiralled into a demanding urgency that almost broke her fragile control.

'Caid,' she whispered, the single syllable a long, heated caress against his mouth.

'Yes, it's all right,' he murmured, 'just relax…'

This time there was no unhurried seduction; desperate, famished, their mouths met in a starving compulsion that blocked everything but the taste of Caid. He didn't move; although she missed the untamed power of his body as the kiss overwhelmed her, the frightened adolescent that still cowered deep inside her welcomed his restraint.

His head lifted a fraction; in a rough, ragged voice he said something so frankly carnal she should have blushed and run. Instead she dipped her head and licked the strong, brown column of his throat, savouring the male musk and spice.

He froze; she could feel his contained breath in the tense cage of his ribs. Smiling secretly, she kissed the pulse beating rapidly at the base of his throat.

Caid's hands slid down her back, came to rest on her hips, pulled her into him with a slight rocking movement. His body was taut and ready and claimant; she felt herself softening, felt heat and moisture as a clamorous, storm-driven surrender prepared a path for him.

'Is this what you want?' he asked, his voice shockingly charged with an overt sensuality. 'Here? Now? Because it's what I want, Sanchia.'

Deliberately he cupped a small, high breast, his thumb moving with obvious sexual intent over the throbbing centre. Sensation shot from her breast to the core of her body. His heavy-lidded eyes searched her face, their vivid colour emphasised by the flash and fire of arousal.

Swamped by fierce, primal pleasure, Sanchia lifted her head so sharply that it spun. And the erotic mists clouding her brain were torn to shreds, banished by the hard, intent purpose she saw in his face. For a hideous second she saw another man's features imposed over Caid's.

A thin, harsh sound pushed her lips apart; she staggered back, her face paper-white.

Caid let her go; as she stumbled clear he demanded, 'Who was it?'

'I don't know what you mean.' But her tone lacked conviction.

'Who attacked you?'

She dragged a breath into her painful lungs, straightened, put a couple of metres between them. Tell him, common sense commanded, but the words wouldn't come. Great-Aunt Kate had warned her to tell no one, and that prudish command uttered by a reticent, elderly woman still bound Sanchia with the force of an injunction.

'Nobody,' she muttered, icy with dread and humiliation.

'Then perhaps you think that an edge of frustration will push up the price I'm prepared to pay for the Bay,' Caid suggested with courteous, cutting cynicism.

Anger, hot and invigorating, rescued her. Sanchia said disdainfully, 'Is that all you can think of?' Long legs eating up the ground in furious strides as she headed towards the car, she hurled a final, caustic word over her shoulder. 'Money?'

He caught her up within a couple of paces. Coolly, ironically, he said, 'When I'm with you money comes way down the list. I think of how elegant your legs are, how your eyes dilate and smoulder when I kiss you, how exquisitely responsive you are—and I wonder why, in spite of the fact that you want me as much as I want you, you pull away every time.'

'Because I'm not a slave to my appetites,' she shot back, fighting down a reckless impulse to tell him her bitter secret.

His ruthless hand closed over hers, jerked her to face him. 'No?' he murmured, his mouth compressed into a merciless smile.

And he kissed her again.

Seething with a desperate cocktail of anger and thwarted desire, Sanchia had no defence. Yet although they began the kiss as antagonists, the moment their mouths touched she went up like wildfire, catapulted mindlessly into a suffocatingly sensual universe where nothing mattered, nothing existed except Caid.

And just before the fear kicked in she was free, and he was smiling dangerously down at her. He was also breathing faster than usual, his chest rising and falling as colour flared along his cheekbones.

'It seems,' he said, stepping back, 'that neither of us should make such a claim.'

Silently they got into the car; silently Caid drove back down the road. But instead of heading home he turned inland.

'Are we going the scenic route?' Sanchia asked remotely.

'I want to call on a friend.'

His tone didn't encourage further questions. Sanchia tried to suspend thought, to empty out her mind, scour it free of the lingering fumes of desire. She wasn't ready to face the significance of what had happened on the beach, except that once again she hadn't been able to bring herself to tell him why she'd never be able to yield to any man.

Coward.

Yet old shame, old dread, chilled her bone-deep at the mere thought of explaining.

She stared straight ahead at hills covered in bush. If Caid loved her, she thought painfully, then she might be able to face the past.

But he'd never said anything about love. Not three years ago, and not now. He'd spoken of desire and attraction and wanting, but the L word had never passed his lips.

All he felt for her was physical hunger, so why would he want to stay when it could never be satisfied? Marriages—even good marriages—had failed under such a burden.

Better to protect herself, to hold aloof, to refuse any more of those heated kisses.

The road led to a marae, a cluster of buildings around a sacred, ceremonial space that was the meeting place and focus of the local Maori community.

In the empty car park they were hailed by an elderly man. Striding across, he greeted Caid by name, beaming as he pumped Caid's hand.

'How are you, boy?' he asked, letting Caid go to stand back and gaze at him. 'It's been too long since we saw you last, and you've got a few more lines than you had then. You work too hard.'

'I don't need to ask how you are,' Caid said with a smile. 'You look fit enough to chase a goat over the Southern Alps. Sanchia, this is Ken Hohua. Ken, a friend of mine, Sanchia Smith.'

Oddly thrilled by such a description, Sanchia shook hands with the elder, colouring as she met his perceptive eyes. 'How do you do, Mr Hohua?'

He said gallantly, 'All the better for seeing you today. Come home, both of you, and have a cup of tea with my wife and me.'

Ten minutes later they were seated in his house while his wife whipped a batch of scones from her oven and made them tea. After they'd drunk the tea and eaten the feather-light scones—and Mrs Hohua had given Sanchia her special recipe for them and the tamarillo jam she'd spread on them—they discussed politics for half an hour or so before they were taken to a housing development within the marae.

'It's our papakainga, the place where our old people live,' Ken explained to Sanchia. 'We needed the houses, but we didn't like the ones we could have bought; we wanted them to be as self-sufficient as possible, so one day we faxed Caid and asked him how to go about it.' He grinned. 'I expected to be fobbed off with an underling, but the next day in comes this helicopter and Caid steps off it and says, "OK, you want houses. Let's deal." He's a tough man, but now we've got our houses and Caid's learned how to cope with Maori protocol.' He laughed up at Caid.

'Jabber, jabber, jabber,' Caid returned cheerfully. 'Meeting after meeting until everyone's had their say.'

'That's the way we do things, and we get there in the end.' The older man winked at Sanchia. 'He doesn't take any nonsense, this boy, but he's well-named—he's got the patience a hunter needs.'

On the way home Sanchia said, 'From the way Mr Hohua was talking, the marae housing is a personal project of yours.'

'I thought it was an excellent idea.' His tone gave nothing away.

'Why did they approach you?'

'Apparently Ken had read an article about a village we worked with in Fiji. He thought we could probably do business, and he was right.' Caid sent her a lop-sided smile. 'We make a profit and they get the sort of houses they want so everyone's happy.'

Did he have to be so public-spirited? To keep her eyes off his lean hands on the wheel and her mind off the kisses they'd shared, Sanchia asked more questions. Judging by the mocking note in his answers he knew what she was doing, but the subject filled the time until they reached the Bay.

They were met by Terry. 'You've had a phone call from the insurance company,' she told Sanchia. 'Here's the number and a name.'

Ten minutes later Sanchia put the receiver down and stood staring blindly at her hands until a knock on the door propelled her across the room. 'Come in,' she said thinly.

Of course it was Caid, his face hardening as he saw her. 'What's the matter?' he demanded, striding across the room.

'The bach is not insured.' She cleared her throat and shrugged. 'Apparently Great-Aunt Kate stopped paying the premiums a couple of years ago.'

Caid said something short and unrepeatable under his breath, then stunned her by walking behind her. Lean hands massaged her neck and shoulders until her knotted muscles began to relax. He pulled her back to rest against him; for a few precious moments she let herself relax against his heat and strength, but almost immediately she straightened up.

He said, 'You'd better sleep on it before you even think about what to do next. For now, come and have some afternoon tea.'

He was kind to her for the rest of the day, a little aloof, but pleasant; he didn't mention the bach or the Bay.

That night Sanchia went to bed early. She tried to read, but eventually put the book down and wondered whether the Caid she'd seen that day, a man with a social conscience, was the real Caid. Had he taken her to Macgregor's Bay and the marae hoping to change her mind about him, hoping she'd decide that he was a suitable owner for Waiora Bay?

She realised she was flipping the pages of the book as though looking for a certain word, a certain scene. 'Will the real Caid Hunter please stand up?' she murmured satirically, closing the volume and putting it on the bed-side table.

She'd never know whether he'd tried to ma-nipulate her, just as she'd never forget what it felt like to be kissed by him.

Three years previously she'd learned to love him, only to discover that the terror embedded in her past doomed any chance of sexual ful-filment.

She still loved him. And it was still utterly hopeless.

Aching with despair, she turned over and pushed her face into the pillow, trying to empty her mind of everything. But after a

while she set her jaw. All right, so she had to
give up her forlorn hope of a sexual relationship, but she could at least overcome this
childish terror and tell Caid the reason she
couldn't make love with him.

And once she'd done that—after she'd met
the man from the District Council tomorrow,
she promised herself—she'd go back to
Auckland and never see him again.

She switched off the light and lay back
against the pillows, only to slide into dreams
of cruel masculine laughter and grasping
hands, of her desperate, panic-stricken fighting, and then of Cathy screaming at her...

Shaking with revulsion, almost suffocating
with old fears and rage, she clawed her way
out of bed and staggered across the room and
out onto the terrace. It took a moment for the
crackling sounds—gunshots?—to register.

No, not gunfire; a heavy stench of smoke
made her cough, and behind the trees a weaving, bobbing patch of light—vivid scarlet and
gold—warned of fire.

She was running across her bedroom when
the door from the passage was wrenched open.

Caid said curtly, 'The bach is on fire. I've rung the brigade.'

A low, indistinct sound burst roughly from her throat. At the sudden blast of the centre light she clamped her eyes shut, blocking out the sight of him in jeans and nothing else.

'They'll be too late,' she said hoarsely.

'I suppose it's no use asking you to stay here?'

She sent him an anguished look and he nodded, his face a grim, hard mask. 'No, I thought not. Get dressed, then—jeans, and something long-sleeved so you don't get burned by sparks.'

'A sweatshirt?'

'All right,' he said, as though giving her permission, and turned and left her.

By the time she got outside the bach had become an inferno. But more alarming than that were the glinting sparks that swirled high into the hot air. Wherever they landed thin, golden lines of fire began to eat greedily through the grass—and soon the bush, the pohutukawas and the butterflies would burn.

She raced along the terrace; ahead of her the mingled silver and scarlet of moonlight and firelight washed across Caid, glimmering across his hair and the smooth, powerful curves of his shoulders when he ran down the steps. Stifling a half-sob, Sanchia followed him.

As they came out onto the beach a car roared down the hill, closely followed by another, and then, thank God, a fire engine.

Caid grabbed her. 'Damn it, Sanchia, stay back!'

'There's no water!'

'They'll run a hose from the fire engine down to the beach.' Ruthlessly he held her in the hard circle of his arms. 'I've got sacks— we'll wet them in the sea and put the grassfire out.'

At that moment the roof fell in a chaos of fire and flames and noise. A searing wind drove a hissing cloud of sparks across the grass.

'Will's bringing shovels, and Pat will be here soon with more shovels and a horde of relatives,' Caid said harshly. 'Pull yourself together; we'll concentrate on saving the bush and the pohutukawas.'

'Yes,' she said numbly. 'I'm sorry.'

He dropped a fierce kiss on her mouth. 'It might look like the end of the world, but it's not,' he said. 'Let's get to work.'

Sanchia never really remembered the order of events after that. All she could summon were images of Mrs Hunter and Terry and Molly Henley running up and down beneath the pohutukawas, wetting a never-ending stream of dry sacks in the sea, of neighbours arriving with spades and shovels, of smoke and fire, harsh and acrid in her nose and throat, of the weariness that eventually turned to pain in her shoulders and arms as she beat out flames. She could recall men working under Caid's direction to contain the avid rivulets of fire that threatened the bush and the trees, and Caid, always Caid, seemingly tireless, working like a demon...

In the end they saved the bush and the pohutukawa trees, but that was all.

'I'll leave a group to watch in case there are any hotspots,' the fire chief said, her face streaked with grime after drinking the last of the coffee and eating two of the sandwiches Mrs Hunter and Terry had organised.

She looked around at the volunteer firefighters and the neighbours who'd come to help, their teeth gleaming in soot-darkened faces as they demolished the coffee and food.

'I'll stay,' Sanchia croaked.

Caid said, 'You will not.' He laid a hand on her shoulder. 'You've done enough.'

'More than enough,' the fire chief said.

Sanchia said, 'If I'd noticed that the guttering had failed there'd have been water in the tank.'

'It wouldn't have saved the bach,' the older woman told her. 'That went up like a rocket.'

Something in her tone alerted Sanchia; she looked up sharply, but before she had time to speak Caid asked curtly, 'Do you suspect arson?'

The woman looked at him, then nodded.

'Why?'

'I'd rather not say at the moment. It'll be inspected tomorrow and we'll know for certain then.'

The hand on Sanchia's shoulder tightened. 'I'll stay down here tonight too,' Caid said.

'No need,' the fire chief said. 'My lot know what to do. You've worked like a Trojan, you and Sanchia. All of you.' She gave a tired smile. 'Thanks. Now go home to bed. Just watch for any signs of smoke inhalation—if you have any difficulty breathing in the next few hours, get to the hospital straight away.'

Back at the house, Mrs Hunter said firmly, 'Bed for you, Sanchia.' She took Sanchia's arm and led her to her room. 'My poor girl, this is a sad time, but don't worry, Caid will make sure everything is all right for you.'

What would it be like to trust someone so much?

Dutifully Sanchia showered again, washing her hair with the expensive shampoo she found beneath the basin, lathering herself with an exquisitely perfumed soap that melted the soot and ashes and smoke from her body. For long moments she stood with the water beating onto her shoulders and arms, soothing the smart of stretched and aching muscles, although tomorrow she'd be so stiff she probably wouldn't be able to do more than hobble, and she had a couple of sore patches where sparks had landed.

Naked, she switched on the hairdryer, slowly lifting the black strands with a brush until they fanned out around her head. Almost groaning with pleasure at the thought of collapsing into bed, she pulled her nightgown over her head and lay down. Sleep engulfed her like a dark tide.

She didn't dream, although in her sleep she was aware of an intense, aching loneliness and emptiness so cold and dark she shuddered with it. Eventually images began to form in the void of her mind—of the cyclone, the hideous noise of the screaming wind, the spume of the towering waves above the broken, beaten hull of the yacht, the dwindling figures of her parents on the deck as she wept silently in the sling beneath the helicopter because she was never going to see them again...

And then warmth enveloped her, and comfort. Astonished, joyous, she saw her parents get up from the deck; the killing waves died down to a moonpath across a gentle sea. Smiling, waving to her, her mother and father blew a final kiss before turning away and walking hand in hand along the glimmering pathway.

She wept again, but this time it was with something like happiness, and in her exhaustion she thought she heard them say goodbye, tell her to be happy, that they loved her and always would.

Slowly, her muscles protesting even in sleep, she turned to the source of the warmth that enveloped her, and in the way dreams work, her parents faded into the brilliant blue of a summer's day, the blue of Caid's eyes.

Even in her sleep Sanchia recognised this for wish-fulfilment, and smiled. In her dream she lay in Caid's arms, against Caid's chest, his warmth enveloping her like a blanket, and in her dream she felt not the slightest flicker of fear. No, in her dream she was bold, she was passionate, she was a worthy mate for such a virile man.

Freed by imagination from the prison of reality, she whispered his name and kissed the hard line of his jaw, her lips lingering over the fascinating abrasion of his beard before moving. Although his heart beat heavily, unevenly, against her, he lay still in the cocoon of the bedclothes, his long, powerful body hers and hers alone in the sanctuary of her mind, of her sleep.

Nuzzling, seeking, she moved her mouth over his face, learning the angular features by touch, sinking into heated hunger as she kissed the fans of his lashes, the straight black brows, the arrogant sweep of his cheekbones.

His scent filled her nostrils, his taste her mouth, all male with a hint of soap, a hint of smoke. Beneath her questing lips his skin was hot and taut.

Finally, when she had imprinted his face, she touched his mouth slowly, softly, shaping its contours with tiny kisses before tracing them with the tip of her tongue. His lips softened beneath hers, matched the kisses she gave him, slow for her slow, fast for her fast, gentle when she wanted them that way, and hard and swift when she plucked up the courage.

Because this was a dream she had all the courage in the world!

She opened her mouth onto his; his immediate, open response sent a jolt of unashamed desire through every cell in her body. Only in a dream, she thought dazedly as she explored the depths of his mouth, could she surrender that small advantage and take his surrender—only in a dream could she thrill to this pure charge of sexuality. It rocketed through her like a maddening hunger, like a charmed delirium.

Made bolder, she touched his chest, felt his skin tighten beneath her fingers. Smiling, she spread her fingers through the tangle of fine hair there, rejoicing at the uneven, heavy thud of his heart against her palm. It travelled through her fingertips and up her arm to reach her own heart, joining it in a rhythm as old as time, as old as passion.

His chest lifted abruptly and then fell; she heard his harsh breath, and lowered her head to kiss the place her palm had rested against, then kissed him again, explored the strong, tense cage of his ribs with her lips and her hand.

Slick, taut beneath her mouth, his skin tasted like Caid—darkly mysterious, the taste of love. Apart from the movement of his breathing, he didn't stir. But why should he? This was a dream, a passionate enchantment she controlled. The realisation gave her the fresh courage to explore further, to push down thin cotton shorts and discover lean hips, strongly muscled flanks.

And between them a shaft of iron sheathed in the slickest silk.

Snatching her hand away, Sanchia sucked in her breath and waited for terror. None came; instead her body thrummed with excitement, with eager, urgent anticipation that ran like heated, spicy wine through her veins, so pleasurable it came close to torment. She ached for something, and her body knew what that something was.

This was her dream, she thought staunchly. She could do what she liked in it. Breathlessly she brushed that strong shaft again. Caid flinched, but he didn't move.

Driven by instinct, by need and love, she sat up and pushed the bedclothes back. With night-accustomed eyes she gazed at him; his eyes were closed, his face harshly shadowed, but his hands lay beside his sides.

Obscurely reassured, she straddled him, hugging his muscled flanks with her thighs. Still he stayed motionless. Slowly, carefully, she lowered herself onto that proud shaft. Her breathing echoed raggedly in the room, drowning out everything but the sound of her heart drumming in her ears.

She slid slowly, deliciously down, astonished at how simple it all was. Simple—yet not
easy. She gasped as the unused muscles in her
inner parts stretched around him, easing, shifting to give him complete access.

For several frowning seconds she froze, until some instinct persuaded her to rock back
and forth a little. That set up a delicious subtle
friction that brought another gasp to her lips.
Tentatively, carefully, she moved her hips
again. Sensation simmered through her, no
longer carefully wooing but urgent, hot and
heavy and demanding. Using her hips and her
thighs and those unsuspected inner muscles,
she pulled him into her and clasped him, and
moulded him deep inside her.

Caid opened his eyes; his arms, so lax at his
sides, moved with shocking suddenness to
grab the headboard of the bed. By now totally
in thrall to passion, Sanchia watched as cords
stood out on either side of his neck, as his arms
and shoulders flexed in what seemed an agony
of waiting. A feverish tide surged through her,
gathering up every sensation, every hint from
every nerve-end, joining and weaving them to-

gether into an overwhelming current of pleasure.

And yet she wanted more, and more, and
more.

Her breath broke hard and fast through her
lips as she coaxed that tide along until it became an irresistible force. Dimly, almost as
though she was awake, she heard herself cry
his name, and then rapture surged through her,
spinning her out of this world into some un-
reachable peak of existence.

As she hit that height she felt Caid stiffen
beneath her, and he groaned, a long, savage
sound that tipped her over the edge and into
ecstasy.

Exhausted, her limbs locked, she came
down with him, her eyelids already closing,
her mind overdosed on pleasure and so thick
and woolly she could barely form the words.
'Ironic, isn't it? I can only do this in dreams...'

She woke late, the angle of the sunlight
through uncurtained windows indicating that
half the morning must have gone by while she
lay in the aftermath of the first erotic dream
she'd ever had.

Stretching limbs still painful from the night's work on the fire, she wondered how on earth she was ever going to look Caid in the eye, let alone tell him why she had to leave, why there could never be any sort of future for them.

More than anything she wanted to take refuge in sleep, but after allowing herself a painfully pleasurable memory of that incredibly erotic dream she got up and showered.

Clad in her thin cotton dressing gown, she was halfway across the room when a sharp tap on the door froze her in mid-step; with her breath bottled in her lungs, she listened.

Make it Mrs Hunter, she prayed childishly. Or Terry. 'Yes?'

'Open up.' Neither Mrs Hunter nor Terry.

Biting her lip, she went across and pushed the door barely open.

Barefoot, clad only in clean jeans and a thin white T-shirt, Caid looked her over unsparingly before asking, 'How are you?'

'My eyes are red and my throat feels like sandpaper, but apart from that I'm fine.' She yawned, a primitive protection against the intensity of his gaze. Adrenalin mainlined through her, banishing tiredness. Dizzily she reined back her reaction to the faint fragrance of soap and clean man, the overt male presence.

He looked tired, as though he'd spent the night awake—or making love. Colour surged up through Sanchia's skin.

His eyes narrowed. 'You're burnt.' A long forefinger hovered above a tender welt on her jawbone, indicated another on her shoulder by the hollow of her throat.

It said a lot for instinct, especially the one concerned with perpetuating the species, she thought wildly, that every cell in her body leapt to meet his touch. Or perhaps she was still lost in the hazy delights of that powerful dream. 'They're nothing—just a few sparks. I ran cold water over myself for five minutes or so last night.'

'I'll get some aloe vera gel. It will stop them blistering.'

She should have spent the time he was away scrambling into some clothes, but that draining lethargy slowed her down so that when he returned she was still in her dressing gown. He was carrying a tray on which was a glass half filled with amber liquid, and a pot of green jelly.

'Lemon and honey,' he said calmly, putting the glass into her hand, 'for your throat. Old Greek recipe, according to my mother. Drink it up and I'll put gel on the bits you can't reach.'

Gratefully she sipped the tangy liquid, sweet and sour combined, letting it run down her arid throat. Caid moved behind her and began to smooth the green gel onto the spark spots on her shoulder; when she shivered he said cryptically, 'Odd how it's always icy, isn't it? It's extremely good for preventing scars.'

Nothing would fade the scars from her past, she thought bleakly. But she'd deal with it, as she'd dealt with everything else in her life— as she'd deal with this ferocious awareness that was roaring through her now, submerging grief and aching tiredness in a desire that threatened to rage into another sort of fire, even more dangerous than the one that had swallowed the bach.

Futile desire, futile need, futile love.

'Drink up,' Caid ordered.

'Have you had any?'

After a moment he said, 'No.'

'You inhaled just as much smoke as I did. More, actually—you were working like a demon to save the bush.' She'd never forget the easy rhythm of his actions, the graceful silhouette against the burning bach as he'd beaten out the fires in the dry grass.

Swallowing, she turned around and held out the glass to him. 'Have the rest—I've drunk enough.' She frowned as she noticed a patch of red skin across one cheekbone. 'You haven't put any of this on your face—let me look.'

His brows lifted; a light kindled in the blue eyes. Sanchia sucked air into famished lungs.

'All right,' he said, handing over the ointment. He took the glass from her and drank some of the liquid.

Sanchia dipped her finger into the pot and moved around him, examining telltale marks on his arms and throat.

Last night she'd dreamed about him, and she'd dreamed accurately. Heart throbbing in a primitive rhythm, she spread the cool gel wherever she saw the marks of fire, making each stroke a tiny caress.

The sparks had only reached his hands and around his neck and face, but she said, 'Just bend down a bit, will you?' Her voice sounded odd—distant, almost breathless.

He paused—it was impossible to think of him hesitating—before stooping towards her. Sanchia found a couple on the back of his neck. 'Honourable wounds,' she said, anointing them.

Straightening abruptly, Caid took the pot of gel and set it and the empty glass down onto a table. His eyes darkened to the colour of a stormy midnight.

'Making love to me last night,' he said, incredibly, 'wasn't a dream, Sanchia. It happened.'

CHAPTER EIGHT

'No,' SANCHIA croaked.

Caid said calmly, 'It happened, Sanchia.'

She had to accept it. Seared by humiliation, she demanded fiercely, 'What were you doing in my bed?'

'I spent a couple of hours down at the bach with the firemen, and then, when it was obvious there were no hotspots to worry about, I came home and showered. I heard you cry out, but when I came in you were so deeply asleep I couldn't shake you out of the nightmare.'

Enigmatic eyes met hers, giving nothing away.

'So I slid into bed beside you,' he said steadily. 'You came into my arms as though you belonged there, and quietened down. And we both went to sleep. For a while.'

Scarlet, she clamped her eyes shut so that she wouldn't have to look at him. 'Oh, God,' she said harshly. 'Why didn't you stop me? *Why didn't you stop me?*'

He paused before saying in a cool, inflexible voice, 'Tell me about the man who attacked you.'

Moving slowly, Sanchia walked across to the side of the bed and sat down on it. 'How did you know?'

'Three years ago you kissed me like a shy houri, passionate and sweet and eager; I realised you'd had very little experience so I went as slowly and carefully as I could, but I always felt a barrier. And when you ran away and left behind a cowardly, prim little letter saying you didn't want to see me again, I asked your great-aunt—'

Sanchia made a sharp, indeterminate noise and flashed him a swift look.

Correctly reading her response, he said levelly, 'Yes, I suspected she hadn't told you anything about that conversation.'

It was impossible to tell what he was thinking or feeling; this was how he must seem to his business associates—remote, awesomely self-reliant, the handsome face a mask for his deeper emotions.

Without inflection he went on, 'She pointed out that you'd made your decision, and any attempt to follow you would be harassment.' After a moment's pause he added drily, 'And she was right. Your rejection was final and more than definite, so I didn't do what I wanted.'

'Which was?'

'Come after you,' he said casually. 'When you arrived the other day, I wanted you the moment I set eyes on you again, and as soon as I touched you I knew you wanted me.'

Astounded, Sanchia shook her head. Heat coloured her skin, dried her mouth. Of course he'd seen the signs of her arousal, and he was too astute not to have read them correctly.

His uncompromising voice went on, 'Yet even when you kissed me the barrier was still firmly in place, as though you were waiting for something to happen, something you dreaded. A sexual attack some time in the past seemed a logical reason.'

Sweat sprang out along Sanchia's brows, beaded across her nose and down her back. 'Yes,' she said.

A killing rage blasted through Caid; he had to discipline his voice to a level, almost un-

interested tone. 'Had you ever made love before last night?'

'No.'

Caid barely heard the monosyllable. He
paused, then said quietly, 'If I'd realised you
were asleep, I'd have woken you, but I was
asleep too. And when I did wake up—believe
me, Sanchia, the last thing I wanted to do was
fight you off. Hell, I couldn't! Besides, you
seemed to know exactly what you were doing.
You even had your eyes open. It wasn't until
you told me it was all a dream that I realised
what had happened. And I can't regret it—
apart from being one of the more transcendental experiences of my life, at least you know
now that you can make love without terror and
pain.'

Her black head drooped on her slender neck,
hiding her face.

Fighting an overpowering urge to protect
her, he coaxed gently, 'Tell me what happened.'

He thought she wasn't going to answer, but
after several taut, silent moments she said in a
subdued, expressionless voice, 'He was

Cathy—my aunt's—boyfriend when I went to live with her after my parents died.'

She hadn't even been thirteen. Choking back the black rage that curled his fingers, Caid spoke slowly and calmly. 'What was his name?'

'Robert Atkins.' Her hands writhed in her lap; she clenched them together and shivered.

Caid bit back an obscenity. No wonder she'd looked sick when he'd told her Cathy was married to the man.

Uneasily he wondered whether he should have called in professional help. Last night, in that half-dazed state between waking and sleeping, he hadn't been able to control his responses to her innocent seduction. It had been a dream-like enslavement, a fantasy that had hovered at the back of his mind for years, and he'd surrendered to it.

This morning he'd been sure that letting her fulfil her desire could only have helped her.

If he'd been wrong, if it had damaged her further, he'd make sure she got help. But first he had to see whether she hated his touch.

Odd how much determination it took to walk across to the bed.

'Sanchia, look at me,' he commanded, crouching down beside her so that their faces were level.

But the big eyes slid sideways, avoiding his. When she spoke it was so softly he could hardly hear her. 'She called him Robbie,' she said.

Gripped by a sudden fear, he controlled it and asked in a calm, level voice, 'What did he do?'

Her eyes darkened and he hoped for a moment that she was going to cry. He could deal with tears.

But although her voice trembled, she said clearly enough, 'He used to touch me. I hated it, but he—I didn't know how to deal with it. I had no one to talk to. He—he threatened me.'

Caid covered her hands with his, clasping them. The pale, slender, competent fingers quivered in his, but at least she didn't flinch.

He thought savagely that he could probably have hit her and she wouldn't have noticed. Her green eyes were opaque, and the woman who'd driven him mad with desire and angry suspicion had gone, leaving a powerless wraith in her place.

She said, 'Then one night he came into my room when I was getting ready for bed and tried to—he held me down with an arm across my throat and—'

Her skin was milk-white, as white as her lips, with great dark smudges under her eyes like bruises. Caid remembered the girl who'd come to Waiora Bay, a child with a child's heartbreaking innocence.

He fought back the low growl at the back of his throat.

Still in the same toneless voice she went on, 'He grabbed at my breasts and—'

'You don't need to tell me this,' he cut in, appalled at having made her relive such horror.

Her great, empty eyes returned to their hands intertwined in her lap. 'My father had taught me how to look after myself. When I tried to gouge his eyes out he yelled and let me go, and Cathy came in and threw me out of the house.'

'She threw *you* out?' Mingled with the disgust and raw fury in his tone was complete disbelief.

Sanchia shrugged. 'He was her meal ticket, whereas I was a constant drain on her finances.' Her voice was steady, toneless. 'I spent three nights hiding in a park nearby, stealing food, before Great-Aunt Kate found me.'

'How did she know you'd run away?'

He watched the muscles move in her long, slender throat as she swallowed. 'She rang to wish me a happy birthday. When Cathy couldn't produce me she came down to Auckland and started searching.'

'Did you tell her what happened?'

Sanchia nodded. 'She said to forget it, that it was over, and she took me away from all that ugliness and became my legal guardian, even though a traumatised kid must have been the last person she'd choose to live with. She gave me back my life, Caid.'

Whereas Cathy and Robert Atkins, Caid thought with narrowed eyes, were about to have their lives severely disrupted.

The violence of his anger drove him to his feet, but he couldn't work off the adrenalin yet; he looked down at Sanchia and saw her stiffen her shoulders and lift her head in a gallant movement that ripped through him. Without thinking, he began to work on her tense muscles with his thumbs, hoping to give her some comforting, unsexual contact.

Relief flooded him as he felt a slow easing of tautness beneath his hands.

Yet it was still in that frightening, muted voice that she continued, 'Great-Aunt Kate didn't want to hear what had happened. She told me not to talk about it, not even to think about it, to push it to the back of my mind. So I did. Then, three years ago—after that summer with you—I went to a therapist. She helped me a lot, but I still wasn't able to— well, you know.'

'Make love. Well, now you know you can.'

As though his words had touched some inner nerve, she leapt to her feet and swung around, hands clenched at her sides. Colour flamed across her high, aristocratic cheekbones.

'Is that why you didn't stop me? Because you thought it would get rid of this inconvenient complex I'd developed?'

How to handle this? He decided to go with instinct, shooting back just as tersely, 'I told you, by the time I realised what was happening it was too late to stop.'

All he'd been able to do was make sure he didn't terrify her with the force of his response, and she'd never know how much self-control he'd had to call up for that.

Sanchia almost exploded with sudden, reviving rage. He'd hesitated just too long before he'd answered her question. Surely he hadn't let her use him like some sort of therapeutic sex aid—not because he wanted her, but because he felt sorry for her!

She blurted, 'I thought I was asleep—when I think of what I thought—what I did—' Shame choked her. She rubbed the back of her hand across her mouth.

'Sanchia, don't,' he said deeply, and although she tried to ward him off he took her in his arms and held her still.

But whatever he'd been going to say remained unspoken when someone knocked on the door.

'Sanchia, are you in there?' Terry's voice.

Sanchia stared into the face of the man she'd love until she died.

'Answer her,' he said quietly. 'I've got a call coming through from America in ten minutes. We'll finish this later.' He dropped a

kiss on her forehead, then let her go and without looking back walked out through the open
doors and along the terrace.

'Sanchia?'

'Coming,' Sanchia said weakly.

Terry didn't seem to notice that Sanchia's
world had tipped upside down since they'd last
seen each other. 'Will's just come up from the
bach,' she said. 'He says there's a Mr
Woodward down there who wants to talk to
you.'

'Woodward?' Sanchia frowned. 'Who is
he?'

'No idea, but he seemed to know you.'

Woodward? Oh, hell, *that* Woodward—the
man from the District Council.

At least it would give her something else to
think about besides Caid. 'I'll go on down,'
she said.

Terry grinned. 'Not like that, I hope,' she
said pertly. 'You'll give him a heart attack!'

Sanchia huddled into an inconspicuous skirt
and little shell top the same green as her eyes,
and sneaked off down the cliff path.

Mr Woodward looked and spoke like a bu-
reaucrat, discreet, close-mouthed, his only con-

cession to the summer heat a short-sleeved shirt. He had the survey plan with him, checking it as they walked around the property boundaries.

Back at the bach, he said, 'So the only access to Waiora Bay is across Caid Hunter's property?'

'Yes, but it's a dedicated road, isn't it?' she asked.

He shook his head. 'No, but don't worry about that. Thank you very much for showing me around. It's a magnificent property, and it's very civic-minded of you to want to give it to us. As soon as it's been discussed in Council we'll get back to you.'

Something compelled her to ask, 'What will happen if the Council decide against a reserve here?'

He looked at her for a moment, then said, 'I don't know.'

He drove away and Sanchia walked quietly past the burnt-out shell of the bach. The stench of smoke and wet ashes and burning still hung on the humid air. For long moments she stood and said a silent, heartfelt farewell to all that remained of eleven years of her life. The bach wasn't hers—had never been hers. It had only been a temporary haven.

Until then she hadn't allowed herself to think about the implications of what had happened the night before, when she'd swung so giddily from despair to rapture. Caid might be pleased that he'd freed her from a stifling sexual terror, but once he discovered what she planned to do with the Bay, he'd probably throw her out!

Sanchia bent down and picked a blue flower, miraculously unscathed by heat and firemen, from the agapanthus clump. She twirled the simple, bright bloom, and made a decision.

If all Caid wanted was a holiday fling she'd give him that, if she was able. Even though she already knew what the ending would be. Men like Caid, who regularly escorted models and film stars and women with titles, didn't promise everlasting love to women like her.

She turned and walked away, beneath the cool shade of the pohutukawa trees, along the beach and up the cliff path.

Caid met her halfway up; he looked at her keenly, but didn't touch her.

'How did your call from America go?' she asked, wondering whether anyone had told him about Mr Woodward.

'Fine,' he said casually. 'You should have waited until I could come down with you.'

Sanchia gave him a pale smile. 'It's all right,' she said.

Another of those keen glances showed that she hadn't convinced him, and once on the terrace he bullied her gently into a chair beside a round iron table on which Terry had put an antique urn filled with an exuberant arrangement of roses and lilies and foliage. Shaded from the sun by an umbrella, the table and chairs, the flowers, and a tray set with glasses and a glass jug of pale pink juice breathed chic sophistication.

Sanchia said, 'If you gave Terry three pieces of grass and a broken shell from the beach she'd conjure a perfect still-life.'

'Terry's talents are inborn, but she's worked hard to hone them.'

'As you have yours?' Sanchia's voice sounded a brittle note in the lazy air.

'As I have,' he agreed drily. His gaze rested a moment on her mouth before flicking up to capture hers. A challenge blazed in his blue eyes as he drawled, 'What are your talents?'

Although Sanchia's throat was parched she had to force herself to drink, using the fruit juice as a barrier against him until eventually she put the glass down. 'I can read extremely fast,' she parried. 'And I seem to have a knack with Asian languages. Nothing artistic, like your mother's ability to design settings, or Terry's with food and flowers.'

'Perhaps you haven't discovered yours yet.'

Something in his tone brought swift colour to her skin. 'Perhaps,' she said dismissively.

Caid's smile added emphasis to his comment, but he began to talk of his mother's attempts to reproduce a small piece of Europe in New Zealand, and slowly Sanchia relaxed.

'You're too astute,' she said, when the guava juice had almost reached the bottom of her glass. 'How did you know that I needed to sit here and let the sun warm me again? I suppose an excellent understanding of human nature is very useful for high-powered businessmen.'

His mouth straightened. 'For anyone,' he said, deflecting the sting in the comment.

Sunlight danced along the rim of her empty glass, shimmering and breaking up into a rainbow before reforming. Keeping her eyes on it, she said, 'Another of your talents is to create beautiful places. The development at Macgregor's Bay is lovely, and so are the marae houses.'

'They were designed by a woman who reminds me a bit of you—Lecia Spring. She's extremely good.' His mouth curved. 'Stroppy and forthright and interesting.'

A dark turbulence arrowed through Sanchia.

'And very happily married,' he finished blandly.

Flushing, Sanchia said lightly, 'She's lucky.'

'She and her husband look alike—a freakish similarity, because the single ancestor they share lived well over a century ago. Their three children, however, look nothing like them and nothing like each other.'

'Genes are strange things,' Sanchia said, her awkwardness concealed, she hoped, by her matter-of-fact tone. For a violent couple of seconds she'd been torn by jealousy—and he knew it.

Need clutched Caid's gut as he watched her. The sun caught her lashes, gilding the tips, casting shifting shadows on her exquisite skin. Her mouth had softened into a sensuous bow; his skin flexed as he recalled the way it felt on him. Curbing his fierce response, he said casually, 'I have my father's colouring and my mother's bone structure. Which of your parents do you look like?'

'Neither. My mother called me her changeling.'

He controlled a spurt of anger. 'Why?'

She shrugged, but he saw an echo of remembered pain in the involuntary tightening of her full lips. 'I don't fit into the family portrait album,' she said lightly. 'She didn't mean anything by it.'

'You said she and your father were a devoted couple.'

'They were.'

'Parents like that can make their children feel like outsiders.'

She sent him a startled glance before her lashes fell again. Perhaps his carefully impersonal kindness had loosened her tongue because she said, 'They loved me, but sometimes I felt like the extra one, the third arm.'

'Made worse, I imagine, when your mother chose to die with your father and you found yourself living with a woman who didn't want you.'

Another dismissive shrug of those smooth shoulders set his body alight. She moved with a sinuous grace that signalled the promise of sex. Good sex. Supremely good sex.

His body responded to that thought with a pounding urgency.

'Did I feel abandoned?' she drawled. 'Yes, of course I did. Kids can be thoroughly unreasonable.' She looked directly at him with sombre, sardonic eyes the turbulent, smoky colour of the best greenstone. 'Only the other day I read that—'

Visibly gathering her reserve about her into a cool, impervious shield, she told him of an amusing article about the general self-absorption of teenagers. Frustration bit into him, but although she was rebuilding her defences as fast as she could, he knew now that he could dismantle them.

When she'd finished the anecdote he said casually, 'Speaking of genes, there's a possibility that you might be pregnant. I didn't use any protection last night.'

Colour surged through her translucent skin. 'No,' she said, her voice stiff and distant. 'I have—I'm on the pill.'

When his brows lifted she said even more stiffly, 'I have bad period pains.'

He nodded, surprised at his flash of disappointment. I must, he thought cynically, be getting dynastic urges. But the image of Sanchia blooming with his child stuck in his mind.

The day drowsed on; when the sun's rays probed beneath the umbrella he insisted they move to loungers in the dense shade of the pergola, and for a while Sanchia slept in a fragrant haze of jasmine perfume.

When she woke Caid was still close by, reading a thick sheaf of papers, the focused, clever face intent as his gaze ran rapidly down each one.

Although the glossy leaves of the jasmine sheltered them, he seemed to glow with an inner light, golden and powerful. He was,

Sanchia thought dreamily, utterly gorgeous, the strong framework of his face buttressing the powerful male beauty of his features and his colouring.

A sudden desire to stretch languorously as a cat hummed through her. Unbidden tides of sensation licked along her nerves, carrying with them secret messages, hidden orders from instincts as old as womankind.

Ignoring them, she sat up. Instantly he stopped reading and glanced across. Her skin tingled, and he smiled and leaned over and kissed her swiftly, his mouth hard and subtly possessive.

Sanchia responded with violent demand, forgetting everything but this dark enchantment of the senses. His mouth moved the length of her throat; pushing aside the shell top he kissed the gentle swell of her breast.

Sanchia waited for the panic, but it was truly gone.

'Touch me,' he murmured against her breast. Heat dissolved her bones, burst through her skin, but a movement in the doorway of the house caught the corner of her eye and she jerked back.

'So here you are!' Clearly rejuvenated, Mrs Hunter smiled benignly at them both.

'She has an instinct for making an entrance too,' Caid murmured mockingly, getting to his feet.

For the rest of the day Sanchia tried to relax, but immediately after a dinner that surpassed even Terry's high standards she excused herself and went to her room. There she stood for a moment, looking around; she'd left the room so quickly she hadn't made the bed, but Terry had done it, and tidied up after her. The clothes she'd worn to fight the grass fire last night had been washed and put away, and the bathroom was immaculate.

In some ways life for the very rich was like a fairy tale.

Slowly, moving like a woman in a dream, she showered with the exquisite toiletries, rubbed her tingling body dry and got into a fine T-shirt.

For the first time in her life she wished she had a silken nightgown, something sensuous and bias-cut that hugged her body, something smokily green, or the same transparent white as her skin.

When she was ready she walked out onto the terrace and sat down in a chair, emptying her mind of everything but the knowledge that Caid would come to her.

Sure enough, when she was night-dazzled and star-dazed, he walked silently across the grass, tall, arrogantly gaited, and stood looking down at her.

'What do you want?' he asked softly.

'You.' Her voice was husky.

'Do you know what you're doing?'

'Yes.'

Sanchia had never been more certain of anything. Elemental needs worked on her; she wanted to lose herself in an emotion bigger than she was, wanted to make memories to hoard against the empty years ahead—the years when Caid would marry a woman more suitable to his position.

But most of all she wanted this man, and the wanting consumed her—wild and sweet, stripped of everything but a stark, elemental need.

Her experiences at Cathy's house had frozen her sexual responses, but perhaps because Caid had kept such a rigorous distance between them during her years with Great-Aunt Kate, she'd allowed herself to fantasise, to daydream that he looked at her as he'd looked at the golden girls he'd shared the holidays with, that he touched her the way he'd touched them...

Long before he kissed her the first time, Caid had found his way through barriers he hadn't known existed. Some time during those long summer days of heat and youth and awareness she'd fallen in love with him, and she'd stayed in love with him.

And last night he'd killed her darkest dragon for her.

'Sanchia?' he prompted, his voice rough, almost threatening. 'I won't let you use me as a comforter to take your mind off the past.'

His next words terrified her.

Holding her gaze, he said, 'Last night was a time out of time, but tonight both of us will know what we're doing. Making love is not like a kiss a mother gives a child to take away the pain or soothe bad memories. It's not comfortable—it's primitive, a basic force of nature, and it changes lives. Is that what you want?'

Some primal part of her quivered, ready to give him what he asked. She put her hand up to run a tentative finger along his cheekbone. Under her fingertip his heated skin was like the finest of leather, supported by the strong framework of his face.

'I don't find you at all comfortable,' she said softly.

He captured her hand and held it prisoner across his mouth. Eyes blazing beneath half-closed eyelids, he said with disturbing intentness, 'The feeling is entirely reciprocal,' and kissed the sensitive palm. While her heart was still rocketing he bit the flesh he'd kissed.

Sensation speared through every cell in her body. Her eyes darkened as she stared at him, her lashes drooping, her mouth softening, becoming fuller, more sensitive.

With a deep laugh Caid pulled her into his arms. But he didn't take her yielding mouth; instead his lips found her pale throat and branded it.

And when he lifted his head he turned her around and kissed the nape of her neck, his hands cupping her breasts. The soft material of her T-shirt abraded her thrusting nipples, but it was the warmth of his hands, their devilish skill, their leashed power that made her gasp. Her head rolled back against his shoulder.

'You're so lovely,' he said in a raw, sensual voice against her skin. 'You walk like the wind, and your skin reminds me of a pearl— translucent, gleaming, white. And your mouth—it's a seduction in itself. Sanchia...'

This, she thought dimly with the small part of her brain still capable of logic, was too much—she craved fire and flash and the oblivion of ecstasy, not this overwhelming tenderness. She wanted the physical drama of sex, the mindless surrender, the blind, feverish passion; she didn't want to be wooed.

But it was, she thought painfully, already too late—she had no chance now of uprooting him from her heart.

Danger crackled through the air, followed his skilful hands. At their touch her bones melted, leaving her lax and unable to move. Caid lifted her and carried her inside and across to the bed; beside it he set her on her feet and eased her T-shirt upwards. She shuddered.

Frowning, he asked, 'Are you all right? Do you want to stop it now?'

Clearly, in spite of the arousal he wasn't trying to hide, he was confident that he could stop if he thought she was afraid.

A twisted pain made her rash. Sanchia wet her lips, her heart singing when she saw how he watched the swift movement of her tongue.

'No,' she croaked. 'I think I'm desperate.'

'So,' he said in a voice raw with need, 'am I.'

CHAPTER NINE

CAID'S reply gave Sanchia the courage to sink onto the bed. Greedily, her hands linked in her lap, she watched him yank off his shirt and strip down his jeans.

Her heart leapt into her throat and blocked it.

Of course she'd seen men without clothes— well, pictures of them; it was practically impossible to grow up without knowing what the naked male form looked like. And over the years she'd seen Caid shirtless, in shorts, in a variety of bathing trunks...

Nothing had prepared her for the reality of Caid without anything covering his beautiful body, not even last night, because last night it had been dark and she'd thought she was dreaming.

Sanchia's breath came rapidly as she feasted on the potent synergy of black hair and taut muscle and the rich, sleek sheen of olive skin, the lethal, masculine grace of strength and litheness. He looked like a Greek sculpture, yet no one would have mistaken him for anything other than a profoundly virile, forceful, dynamic man.

Smooth and as inevitable as flowing honey, an aching languor drenched her. In seething impatience she swung her legs onto the bed and watched from beneath her lashes as he walked around to the other side. Instinct warned her that his prowling desire was firmly caged behind the bars of his will, perhaps because he still wondered about her fitness for this.

Although later she might respect him for his consideration, it was the last thing she wanted now. Their lovemaking the previous night had released her wild inner self from a cage of secrets, freeing a Sanchia with no scars, no inhibitions.

So as he came down beside her she ran questioning fingers across his chest, following the patterned scrolls of hair.

When her seeking hand reached his waist he made a rough noise in his throat. 'Not yet,' he ordered on a half-laugh, easing her back onto the pillows.

Her heart shook, but although this might be the biggest mistake in her life she wasn't going to stop now.

She couldn't. Already her body was softening, the secret inner passageway throbbing with anticipation. Warmth flooded her, and a return of that need to stretch, to twist against him—it was like a fever deep in her bones, yet she welcomed the fiery ache.

His handsome face grave, he surveyed her. Not a muscle moved; she thought he'd retreated to some place where perhaps no woman could reach him. And then he smiled and bent his head and kissed the gentle swell of her breast, and Sanchia went up in flames.

What followed proved that Caid was a brilliant lover—tormentingly generous, touched by greatness, able to wring the utmost sensation from a body only too keen to respond. Sanchia discovered that his lightest caress could knot through her in a pleading, insistent demand that was totally outside her experience.

Under his skilled tutelage her hunger increased to a tempest, a drumming, boundless urgency. When he touched her, when she licked the smooth tanned skin of his shoulder and his taste filled her mouth and clouded her brain, when she writhed against the sheets, her head thrashing back and forth on the pillows as he showed her how ravishing his mouth on her breasts could be, her brain gave up the fight to think. Heavy eyelids drifting down, she let her other senses spring into full play; she smelled their lovemaking, heated, mingled faintly with the musk of the jasmine outside, and she felt...oh, how she felt!

Lost in the erotic slide of skin against skin, the sensations his masterful hands coaxed from her, she found her own power. It both soothed and stimulated some repressed need in her when she realised that her touch made him catch his breath, that he stiffened beneath her hands, that her mouth on his body made him tremble.

When at last he commanded gutturally, 'Open your eyes,' she had to force her lashes upward. She saw a face drawn with passion, the angular framework strained and uncompromising in a stark, determined drive towards completion.

A fierce elation exploded through the heated languor of her bones and body. Smiling, she said thickly, 'It's all right, Caid; I know who you are.'

'And I know who you are,' he said, as though it was a vow, and thrust into the passage that waited for him, that he'd prepared so skilfully.

A terrifying pleasure exploded through her. Linking her hands across the bunched muscles of his back, she opened to him, working to pull him in, lock him against the entrance to her womb in a grip that insisted and entreated and persuaded and promised, a grip as instinctive as it was irresistible.

Eyes narrowed and smouldering, Caid withdrew, only to thrust again and again. She met his need, matched it, joined him in setting up a rhythm that reverberated through her until it gathered in a central place, pouring into her and from her in waves that surged higher and higher, more and more intensely. And then they caught her and tossed her into ecstasy, a rapture so unbearable that she sobbed with its beauty.

Caid followed almost immediately, his head thrown back as he spilled himself into her, a shivering groan torn from his throat. For a fleeting moment she felt his beloved weight on her, before in one fluid movement he turned onto his side and scooped her across him.

Sanchia made a small distressed sound.

'What is it?' he asked, his voice oddly hoarse.

'Nothing.' How could she say she'd wanted to cradle him for a few more precious seconds?

'I'm too heavy to lie on you for long.'

'I don't think so,' she muttered, hiding a huge yawn in his shoulder.

His chest lifted in a half-laugh. 'Trust me,' he said drily. He kissed her on the forehead before threading his hands through her hair to hold up her face. Blue and enigmatic as the depths of space, his eyes searched hers. 'Did I hurt you?'

'You know you didn't.'

That smile caught his mouth. 'No sign of panic?'

When she shook her head he kissed her again and Sanchia, who'd believed passion died with satiation, discovered that it merely slumbered.

'No, not now, not again,' he said in a constricted voice against her mouth. 'You need time to recover. I'd like to lie with you tonight and hold you, but if I stay we'll make love again. You have a powerful effect on me—as you may have noticed.' His smile was wry.

Sanchia sighed. 'It's unfair,' she said sleepily. 'Stay with me.'

'I have to go.'

So that his mother didn't discover he'd slept with her guest?

'Then you'd better go now,' she said, and because she couldn't help herself she kissed the corner of his mouth, and a soft earlobe.

'Don't tempt me,' he said, returning the kiss on her mouth, then got up, magnificently unashamed in his nudity, and pulled his jeans on.

His gaze ran hotly over her body. 'Sleep well,' he said.

When she woke, pleasantly aching, as the bird chorus gathered in the bush to celebrate the dawn, she lay dreamily sorting her memories, filing them into the storehouse of her brain.

Eventually she got out of bed and walked across to the windows, pushing back the curtains.

Oh, God, she thought, closing her eyes on the sky of clear blue sprinkled with feathery silver clouds, last night had been heaven; she loved Caid with everything in her, every part of her.

But when Caid decided to marry he'd choose a woman from his own circle, someone who could take her place in the world of the very rich—someone like the girls who'd used to come to the Bay during the holidays—a sleek, pampered woman with excellent connections, a woman who knew how to organise everything from a dinner party to a charity ball.

Not Sanchia Smith, who had no connections, no influence, and whose idea of a dinner party was an informal occasion with friends!

Struggling to free her brain of obsessive images, of remembered ecstasy, she pushed the door back and breathed in. No smoke sullied the air, but she could still smell the faint stench of burning. Turning away, she headed for the shower.

*　　*　　*

'Did you sleep well last night?' Mrs Hunter looked enquiringly across the breakfast table.

Trying to ignore the colour licking along her cheekbones, Sanchia accepted a cup of coffee. 'Like a log, thank you.' She kept her eyes studiously away from Caid, big and dominant and amused on the other side of the table.

There was something lazily possessive about him this morning; if his mother hadn't already realised what had happened she soon would, Sanchia thought stringently.

Not that she resented his attitude; she too was feeling rather like a cat presented with a particularly succulent canary.

Transferring her attention to her son, Mrs Hunter asked, 'So what are your plans for today, Caid?'

This loving inquisition was part of their breakfast routine. A tiny ache of envy made Sanchia wonder what it would be like to belong to a family again.

Caid shrugged. 'I have some work to do this morning,' he said succinctly. 'After lunch I have a landowners' meeting in Kerikeri. It usually takes the whole afternoon, but if I can get away early I might take the boat out.'

'That sounds delightful,' his mother said in her accented English. 'But not for me. I am going to discuss with Will a new idea I have for the garden.'

Her son grinned at her. 'For someone who grew up on a Greek island you're remarkably resistant to boating,' he teased.

His mother laughed. 'We're notorious for seasickness. As a child I used to wonder how on earth Jason got as far as the Golden Fleece without losing most of his crew! You're lucky—you have your father's constitution. He used to say he had a cast-iron stomach.' Smiling, she turned to Sanchia. 'How well does your stomach behave at sea?'

'Superbly. I grew up on a yacht,' Sanchia told her.

Mrs Hunter nodded. 'Of course, I had forgotten. So what are your plans for today?'

'I don't know,' Sanchia said in a surprised voice. Too busy, she realised guiltily, enjoying memories of Caid's lovemaking to make plans. 'I should do something about the bach.'

'I've already organised for what's left of it to be demolished and removed,' Caid said.

Sanchia protested, 'Oh, but—'

Decisive blue eyes met hers, held them. He said, 'I don't like the smell of burning.'

'Which doesn't make you any less high-handed,' Sanchia shot back.

He leaned back and surveyed her down an arrogant nose. 'It's under way, Sanchia, so there's nothing you can do about it now.'

In a troubled voice Mrs Hunter said, 'When will we know whether or not it was arson?'

'I heard last night.' Caid ignored Sanchia's startled glance. 'It was. Someone lit a fire in the sitting room. The inspector found traces of an accelerant.'

Sanchia felt sick. 'Why would anyone want to burn it down?'

'Vandals enjoy destruction,' he said austerely. 'At least they chose an empty house.'

Mrs Hunter set her coffee cup down with a clink. 'Do you think that the people who burnt it down are the ones Will told us about?'

'What people?' Sanchia demanded.

Caid overrode his mother's explanation pleasantly but firmly. 'A month ago people began gathering on the beach for parties. After a couple of incidents Will and Pat saw them off and secured the gate. There was no further trouble until the night before last.'

But if she went ahead with her plans—with Great-Aunt Kate's plans—the Hunters would have to deal not only with crowds of people on the beach but the possibility of more such incidents. Sanchia's stomach contracted again and she bit her lower lip for a second. 'Perhaps they'll be satisfied now that the bach has gone.'

'Unless they decide to burn down the butterfly tree,' Caid said coolly.

Horrified, Sanchia exclaimed, 'No!'

'Why not?' he said, watching her from eyes half hidden by his heavy lashes. Unspoken was the implication that if she sold it to him there would be no further danger.

He was very good at probing weaknesses; it was probably part of his job description, if the owner of Hunter's wrote himself such a thing. A man who successfully ran a huge company in the volatile world of the Pacific Rim needed ruthlessness as well as powerful self-assurance and dynamic energy. He had them all, along with a formidable intellect and that dynamic power.

Fixing her gaze on a sunbeam playing along the end of her knife, Sanchia said, 'I can't believe that anyone would be so evil.'

Black brows lifted. 'A refreshing—if somewhat naïve—trust in mankind's goodness,' he said, a cutting note sharpening the words. 'Do you want to come into Kerikeri with me this afternoon? You could shop while I go to this meeting.'

'No, thank you,' she said quietly, not meeting his eyes.

'I'm going to see Molly Henley,' Mrs Hunter said, bestowing a smile of warm approval on Sanchia. 'Will you be happy by yourself?'

Sanchia blinked. 'Perfectly,' she said vaguely.

They were eating breakfast on the morning terrace, away from the sea, and on the other side of the house from the blackened ruins of the bach. Flowers danced in the garden—shaggy little suns of gazanias, other blooms that glowed like gaudy, fringed stars in shades of scarlet, gold, magenta and copper, all contrasting with the dramatically surreal blue and orange 'birds' on the bird of paradise bushes.

Mrs Hunter had created another setting, backing a brilliant tapestry of colours with the mingled, scented leaves of lavender and rosemary. Behind the Mediterranean shrubs reared the dark, silver-backed domes of the pohutukawas and the tropical exuberance of trees with huge, paddle-shaped leaves, glossy as enamel in the sunlight.

A transient breeze carried with it an acrid trace of embers. Desolation gripped Sanchia so fiercely that the sunlight dimmed and the riotous colours faded. If she fulfilled the promise she'd made to Great-Aunt Kate, she'd spoil Waiora Bay for both Caid and his mother.

And if she didn't, she'd never forgive herself.

She said, 'I'll go down to the bach and see if there's anything I can salvage.'

Caid's frowning gaze searched her face. 'Nothing could have survived that inferno.'

'I have to make sure.'

'I suppose you do,' he said reluctantly. 'All right, let's go.'

She'd have preferred to be by herself, but clearly that wasn't an option. Caid didn't intrude; silently he stayed beside her as she surveyed the pathetic remnants of the bach. He was right; nothing had been saved.

Tears clogged her throat, gathered in her eyes. Caid turned her into his arms and murmured soothingly; he didn't seem to notice the stirring of his body as she wept into his shoulder, and after a few seconds she relaxed, able to concentrate on her sadness.

She wouldn't let it last; tears provided relief, but they weren't a solution. Caid sensed when she recovered her control almost before she did. Keeping an arm lightly around her shoulder, he offered a large handkerchief.

As she wiped her eyes he said, 'It made a fantastic funeral pyre. I know it hurts now, but she'd have enjoyed it—rather like a Viking going out with his ship.'

Kate Tregear had given sanctuary and love to a young girl. The least that Sanchia could do was achieve her great-aunt's dream.

'She was a fighter,' Sanchia said in a kind of valediction.

For the first time in her life Sanchia had a nap after lunch. It was, she decided on waking, a much overrated exercise. Yawning, a slight headache banging behind her temples, she got into her bathing suit, anointed herself with sunscreen and went in search of a beach towel.

'Yes, you look as though you could do with a dip,' Terry said, handing over a huge bath sheet decorated with a splendid octopus. 'Be careful, though—it's hot out there.'

'I'll take care.'

Swimming had always been a release, the mindless pleasure of cool water against her skin easing pressures and fears. That day it was even more sensuously hypnotic than usual. Had making love with Caid distilled a keener, more physical pleasure within her?

If so, it was completely unfair, she thought bitterly as she waded back onto the beach— like dangling a tantalising promise of paradise in front of her, then whipping it away with a sinister laugh.

The sand was already too hot to be comfortable. After a startled yelp Sanchia raced across the blinding expanse of the beach into the shade of the pohutukawas. She was languidly drying herself down when the hairs on the back of her neck lifted.

Swinging around, she saw Caid striding along the beach. Something about the set of his broad shoulders, the way he walked, told her he was in a towering fury. Surely not because she'd gone swimming by herself?

All fingers and thumbs, she knotted the towel around her waist. Her stomach clenched against an imaginary blow and she braced her shoulders, waiting until he was within earshot before saying neutrally, 'Hello.'

'I've just been talking to Nat Blackmore.' His voice was cold and uncompromising.

'Why did a conversation with the man who owns the cattle station next door make you so angry?'

'Nat used to be a councillor on the District Council, and still has excellent contacts in it.' Caid's deep voice sounded almost indifferent, but there was nothing indifferent about the icy blue fire in his eyes.

Sanchia braced herself for the inevitable. 'So?'

'So he says that you're planning to offer the Bay to the Council as a reserve.'

Heart twisting, she said calmly, 'I've already offered it.'

Speaking with a silky directness that made each word a separate and potent threat, he said, 'You clever, lying, conniving little—'

'I didn't lie!'

'You lied by omission.' Hard contempt vibrated through his voice. The sun emphasised his handsome face, picking out the powerful symmetry of bone structure, the dark, dominant character. A black cotton shirt clung to his torso, and black trousers blatantly revealed powerful thighs.

Sanchia stayed miserably silent, because he was right—she had lied by omission. Her behaviour suddenly seemed cheap and deceitful—and cowardly.

Caid said in a low, furious voice, 'That was a very skilful, clever seduction! I fell for the oldest trick in the book—did you really think I'd be bought off with a couple of nights in your bed, Sanchia? You rate yourself too highly. Your body might well fuel a million erotic dreams, but I don't like women who are greedy, self-serving and debauched enough to prostitute themselves.'

Oh, God, this was so much worse than she'd anticipated. Shock and cold despair made her flinch. 'I didn't seduce you,' she returned. Her voice cracked on a note of strain, but held steady. 'I'll get into some clothes and then we can talk.'

His lip curled and his eyes drifted down the length of her sleek, wet body. 'A good idea.' Insolence purred through his tone, emphasising the taunting male speculation in his gaze.

Inner heat scorching her skin, Sanchia walked past him. 'Unless you change your attitude I've got nothing to say,' she tossed over her shoulder.

'I, however, have a great deal to say, and you're going to listen while I say it.' His voice hardened into tough, relentless authority. 'If you go ahead with this crackpot scheme I won't be the only one to fight you through every court in the country.'

Pain scarred her with its claws. She pushed her wet hair back from her face and said stoutly, 'You can't do anything to stop it.'

The merciless slash of his smile told her what he thought of that. 'As soon as the Council finds out it will be buying into a fight—a long, expensive lawsuit, the sort that sets ratepayers howling for blood—it'll come

up with another way to deal with your offer.
Then there's the question of access to the Bay
across my land. They're pragmatic enough to
accept the Bay as a reserve, Sanchia, but
they'll sell it to me as soon as you're out of
the picture. I'm sure you need that money
more than the Council does.'

'I'll tie it up so they can't,' she said furiously. 'As for the offer of blood money—no,
thank you!'

He gave her a cool, sardonic look. 'Local
councils can do whatever they like with be-
quests.'

It made hideous sense. Sanchia faced him,
her eyes glittering green fire in a white face.
'And you, of course,' she retorted with poi-
sonous sweetness, 'will do anything to stop the
great unwashed public wandering around near
your house.'

'For obvious reasons,' he said forcefully,
nodding towards the gaunt, burnt-out ruins of
the bach.

'I promised Great-Aunt Kate I'd deed it to
the council.'

He looked at her as though she were something he'd scraped off the sole of his shoe.

'You've forgotten that I have a claim on the Bay.'

'What claim?' Ablaze with anger and disillusion, she added intemperately, 'I'm not going against my great-aunt's wishes just because you want to get your greedy hands on her home.'

Between his teeth, he said, 'I still don't know who signed that annuity agreement. However, I've already paid out a hundred and twenty thousand dollars on the place, and until that's settled you won't be able to do anything about the Bay.'

'It's not my debt—and certainly not Great-Aunt Kate's.' Her chin came up as she glared at him. Her debt was to the woman who'd rescued her from hell, the woman who'd trusted her to carry out her final wishes.

Stumbling, she said, 'I'm sorry the value of your property will go down—'

'I don't give a toss about the property value,' he grated. Turning, he gestured at the house on the cliff. 'My mother loves this house because my father built it for her; she comes back here to remember him and restore her spirit.' He swung back and fixed Sanchia with a metallic stare. 'That's why your great-aunt bought the bach and this land—to restore *her* spirit. She didn't want the land to be a reserve while she was still alive to enjoy it. Forgive me if I see an element of selfishness in her bequest.'

'She wasn't selfish!'

'She certainly wasn't perfect. Where the hell are you going?'

'Up to the house,' Sanchia said, stone-faced. 'I'll collect my clothes and leave.'

CHAPTER TEN

CAID said between his teeth, 'Running away, Sanchia?'

Each contemptuous word flicked across her raw nerves. 'I've got nothing more to say to you,' she retorted stiffly.

His lashes drooped to half cover his eyes; he scanned her face then dropped his gaze to her breasts for a searing moment. To her furious embarrassment the centres peaked, thrusting through the thin material of her bathing suit.

At least he didn't say anything beyond, 'You're starting to burn. Come up to the house.'

In taut silence they walked up the cliff path. On the terrace he said, 'Come down to the office with me, please.' A flinty undernote revealed it to be an order, not the request he'd couched it as.

'Certainly,' she said with stoic calmness.

The office was immaculate. An organised man, she thought ironically; she tended to be a piles-on-the-floor sort of person. In the corner a computer hummed, and as Caid closed the door after her the fax grumbled to indicate a message coming through.

He didn't even look at the paper feeding out of the machine. Stopping her with a hand on her arm, he tipped her chin up with a ruthless hand, his eyes scanning her face. 'Why didn't you tell me what you planned to do with the Bay?'

She froze. How could she say that she hadn't wanted to spoil their fragile relationship? He'd laugh, because what sort of relationship did they have? She loved him while he merely wanted her—hardly anything to build dreams on.

'I knew how you'd feel,' she said curtly. 'I didn't need the aggravation.'

His eyes narrowed. 'I suppose you hoped to organise the whole thing behind my back.'

Shame burned her skin.

'You wouldn't have got away with it,' he said coolly, 'because Pat would have told me what you were up to. As for hoping that sleep-

ing with me would stop me from objecting—
you don't know me very well, Sanchia, if you
really believed that.'

Long fingers wrapped gently around her
throat. Angry and ashamed, she looked up into
hooded, dangerous eyes.

'I didn't believe it,' she said through
clenched teeth.

'You resented it when you thought I was
trying to bribe you. I don't bribe either,' he
said, and claimed her mouth in a simple,
straightforward, lustful kiss, possessive and
territorial, that smashed all Sanchia's carefully
built defences.

This would be their last kiss and, by heaven,
she'd make sure he never forgot it! Leaning
into him until they were pressed hip to hip,
thigh to thigh, she surrendered a mouth as hun-
gry as his. A wild, reckless joy rocketed
through her. Kissing Caid was like the promise
of water in the desert, like the cloud on the
horizon that whispers of an island after unbearable days at sea...

Although she wanted nothing more than to
yield entirely, eventually she twisted her head
away to break the contact, forcing the hands

that had clamped across his broad back down to her sides.

When his arms tightened she looked at him with a blank stare and a cold, composed face. 'I'm not going to prostitute myself again,' she said bleakly. Let him think what he liked!

Such anger darkened his eyes that her heart compressed into a dense ball. She heard a low curse in Greek, and tore her gaze from a face as hard as granite.

Watching her through his lashes with dangerous intentness, vivid eyes glittering with a palpable aura of menace, he said, 'I'll tell my mother that you've decided to go home.'

Straightening her spine, reinforcing bones that had melted, she said proudly, 'I'll pack now.'

How ironic that she could only fulfil her promise to her aunt by ruining her relationship with Caid!

An hour later, driving south along the hot, holiday-clogged roads in her small, hot car, Sanchia smiled bitterly. What relationship? 'Sex,' she said out loud, taking evasive action as some halfwit cut in front of her.

At least Caid had been honest—he'd never hinted at anything more.

And for her it had begun as an obsession born of overheated adolescent dreams, then somehow been transformed into love—simple, straightforward, so wonderful that it broke her heart. Hopeless…

She didn't blame Caid for hating the prospect of a reserve next door to his house. With public access came noise, and mess, and occasional wanton destruction; the temptation to give him the Bay was so strong she could feel the bittersweet taste of surrender in her mouth. That final kiss—long, piercingly sweet and textured with peril in spite of the anger behind it—had warned her that she had to get away before she yielded so much to him that she'd never find the way back to herself.

She'd let herself fall into the trap of hope. If he felt anything at all for her beyond a wildfire physical attraction edged by years of repression, he'd have tried to understand why carrying out Great-Aunt Kate's wish was so important to her.

But he didn't want to know. He'd enjoyed her, and no doubt he'd have been happy to indulge in an affair until the novelty palled. Then he'd get on with his life with no regrets.

Just as she had to. Overcoming this secret love was just a matter of distance and time and will-power. Today—right now!—she'd start chiselling away at the image she'd secretly harboured in her heart.

Although she teetered on the edge of an echoing, empty abyss, she had to somehow summon the courage to cross it. In time she might even be able to thank him for so comprehensively demolishing her terror of sex.

Her head jerked up and she squared her shoulders. She'd survive.

Three long, hot weeks later, in Auckland, an assertive peal on the front doorbell brought Sanchia in from the terrace, a fugitive, unbidden excitement channelling through her.

So stupid, because although her brain told her it would never be Caid, her heart still hoped.

She dropped the newspaper she'd been pretending to read onto the sofa in the sitting room. After her flatmates had left for work this hot, humid Auckland day, she'd opened every window and French door and indulged in an orgy of cleaning—anything to take her mind off the reverberating loneliness. It hadn't helped—how did you kill a longing rooted in the very cells of your body?—but at least it had given her something to concentrate on.

Yet although an aching emptiness overshadowed her, she'd achieved a small measure of peace. Since she'd had to choose between Great-Aunt Kate's wishes and Caid's, she understood the fundamental clash of loyalties that had led her mother to die with her husband in the howling wastes of the Pacific. Sanchia had chosen to walk away from the man she loved, but her new understanding appeased a heart-deep sense of abandonment she'd never acknowledged or accepted until then.

Because if Caid had loved her she might have made the same decision and abandoned Great-Aunt Kate's sacred trust.

Another impatient peal on the doorbell urged her along the passage. She opened it, and was pushed back into the hallway. Two people advanced on her—her aunt Cathy, a glittering smile curving her wide, sensual, lightly coloured mouth, eyes as green as

Sanchia's opaque in her beautiful face, and Robert Atkins.

'Hello, Sanchia,' Cathy purred.

Afterwards Sanchia would ask herself why on earth she'd let them herd her down the passage, but locked in a hideous replay of the past she couldn't resist. Slim, honed body swaying beneath a floating white linen dress, Cathy kept smiling and advancing. Beside her, her husband smiled too, but in his face Sanchia read real malevolence.

'What do you want?' The words rasped; she was twelve again, terrified.

'You great, stupid bitch,' Cathy said sweetly, her smile still fixed to her lovely face. 'You couldn't wait to blame me for that annuity, could you? No, you opened that ugly mouth of yours and told Caid Hunter all about your wicked aunt—'

Sanchia swallowed. 'I did not.'

'So who else would have?' Robert Atkins sneered.

Cathy ignored him. 'I'm quite sure Aunt Kate wouldn't have discussed me with Mr Hunter, so it had to be you.'

'And because you couldn't keep your mouth shut,' her husband said savagely, 'we're in the can. You're going to get us out of it, or you're going to pay.'

Until that final gloating word Sanchia had backed away from them, so caught up in the past that she couldn't think, couldn't do anything more than respond with a complete shutdown of intellect and determination.

But she was no longer twelve, alone and afraid. Calling on every shred of will-power she possessed, she turned into the sitting room, walking ahead of them. With a retreat available through the open French windows, she stopped and swung to face them.

A rapid rush of adrenalin revived her as they too halted. 'What the devil do you mean by that?' she demanded, furious with herself for giving them the opportunity to intimidate her. 'I can't get you out of trouble, and there's no way I'm going to pay.'

Robert Atkins said loudly, 'You're going to do what you should have done—what any normal person would have done!—when Kate Tregear died. You're going to sell Caid Hunter the Bay so that he can deduct the money from the purchase price.'

'I'll do no such thing!'

Cathy's smile danced along her mouth. 'Then I'll start proceedings to make a claim on Kate's estate. Think, Sanchia, how much time and money that's going to take—time you can't afford, and money you don't have. Sell to Caid Hunter, and I won't need to do it.'

'You have no legal right to her estate,' Sanchia retorted, 'and you've got a damned nerve, coming here and telling me what to do.' She looked at them with contempt. 'Caid must have really scared you.'

'You little bitch—' Swift as a snake, Robert Atkins grabbed at her.

Sanchia leapt backwards, narrowly avoiding those clutching fingers. Her heart raced, yet that first paralysing terror had vanished completely, replaced by cold, watchful anger. This man, she realised with a wild, reviving thump of relief, the ogre who'd tainted years of her life, was an inch shorter than she was. The years had greyed his head and carved lines into his weakly handsome, dissipated face.

She was no longer afraid of him.

In her curtest tone she said, 'What on earth made you think you could get away with stealing from Caid Hunter, of all people? Did you honestly think he wouldn't find out that he'd paid a hundred and twenty thousand dollars for a fake annuity? Or that when he found out he'd let you get away with it? *Caid Hunter*, known the world over for his killer instinct?'

Cathy said viciously, 'If you'd done what you were supposed to do when Kate died—sell the place—no one would have ever been any wiser.'

'I'd have found out.'

'You wouldn't, and neither would Caid Hunter, because he'd have offered you a price that took the annuity into consideration, and because he's the sort of upright man who'd have obeyed what he believed to be a proud old lady's plea for secrecy. I had everything worked out, and if it hadn't been for you we'd all have been happy. But no, you had to dig in your heels...'

'Fortunately, we know how to apply pressure,' her husband said, smiling, his pale eyes dilating as he eyed Sanchia's breasts.

Remnant fear shivered down her spine, but she asked with cool disdain, 'What pressure can you apply?'

Cathy said tensely, 'I've got nothing to lose, do you understand, you stupid slut? I'm not going to spend years locked away because of your ridiculous devotion to a crazy old woman's whim. If you don't sell the Bay to Caid Hunter I'll make sure you suffer—I'll take everything you value from you, and if that means I have to burn this place down and fire-bomb your car, that's where I'll start.'

It could have been an empty threat, but there was an edge of desperation to her tone and in her face that brought up the tiny hairs on the nape of Sanchia's neck. Trying for time, she asked, 'How did you find out what Great-Aunt Kate wanted to do with the Bay?'

'Caid Hunter told us.' Robert Atkins's mouth worked as though he'd tasted something foul.

Her composure recovered, Cathy gave her a smug glance. 'He suggested that we come and see you,' she purred.

Surely Caid hadn't sent them here to threaten her—no! No, he wanted the Bay, but not that much.

Steadily Sanchia said, 'Even if I wanted to save you from the results of your own greed, I couldn't. I'm not going to sell the Bay and I've got no influence over Caid.'

Cathy gave a tinkling little laugh. 'Oh, for God's sake, you're no raving beauty, but you've got all the equipment! There's no accounting for tastes—even the sexiest magnate might want to go slumming now and then— and it's a rare man who'll turn down what you've got to offer.'

Sickened, Sanchia said evenly, 'Nothing I could do or say would make Caid Hunter change his mind.'

'You haven't changed a bit,' Cathy spat, her façade cracking. 'And all for a measly hundred and twenty thousand dollars. He's a multimillionaire—probably a billionaire by now. He probably spends that amount each year on his handkerchiefs. As for you, you're still a bloody sanctimonious—'

Something behind Sanchia caught Cathy's attention. Her voice stumbled and died, her eyes widening and her skin blanching into a sick pallor.

Sanchia swung nervously around, her incredulous gaze registering the man silhouetted in the open French windows.

She dragged in a deep, ragged breath. The angular lines and planes of Caid's face were like a mask, expressionless, coldly perfect.

'Caid?' she said, her voice mirroring her uncertainty.

Ignoring her, his cold blue gaze fixed on Cathy, he walked into the room and said in a voice so soft it froze Sanchia's blood, 'What the hell do you think you're doing?'

Although her cosmetics stood out so that she looked like a little painted doll, Cathy attempted her usual confident tone. 'We're having a family discussion.'

'It didn't sound like that to me,' he said, with a glance at Robert Atkins that made the other man step back involuntarily. 'You threatened Sanchia.'

Sanchia said unevenly, 'Why are you here?'

His smile didn't reach his eyes. 'This morning I had an interesting interview with your *aunt*—' his voice emphasised the word with contempt '—and her husband. After they left me they were overheard deciding to visit you.'

He hadn't come alone. The man who stood behind him was so inconspicuous that his profession, security expert, was obvious.

Negligently, not trying to hide his cold disdain, Caid continued, 'Get out, you two, and don't come back. I should have expected you to try and force Sanchia to repay the money you owe me, but it's not going to work.'

Cathy and her husband looked at each other.

'Nothing would give me greater pleasure than to hand you over to the police,' Caid told them with chilling disgust. 'Get within fifty yards of Sanchia again, or contact her in any way, and that's what will happen.'

Cathy summoned a smile, a clever blend of respect and female appreciation that paid subtle homage to his overpowering maleness as well as his status.

She kept it pinned to her mouth even when Caid looked at her with eyebrows raised, visibly unimpressed.

Before she could speak Robert Atkins blustered, 'You have no proof.'

'I have a paper trail leading right to you,' Caid said. He looked at the anonymous man,

'Perhaps you could escort Mr and Mrs Atkins out.'

Again Cathy and her husband exchanged glances. After a tight pause Cathy said with a sketch of shrug, 'All right, we'll go quietly.'

'I'll see you later,' Caid said.

Sanchia shivered. He hadn't raised his voice, hadn't altered his stance, but the aura of menace around him had thickened, become almost palpable in the warm, sunny room.

'If it means so much to you,' Cathy said coolly, her eyes flicking to Sanchia's stunned face, 'we'll get out of the country and stay out.'

'An excellent idea,' Caid said. When the room had emptied, he asked, 'Are you all right?'

'Yes.' Sanchia kept her voice level. 'What will you do with them?'

'Don't worry about them,' he said, coolly courteous. 'Promise me that if they get in touch with you again you'll contact me.'

Anything to get him out of there so that she could listen to the sound of her heart breaking in private. 'Certainly,' she said politely.

She even walked with him to the door. But once there she blurted, 'If Cathy's spent all the money she got from you I'll sell you the Bay. At a price that takes the money you've already spent into account.'

Caid's dark brows drew together above unreadable blue eyes as he surveyed her.

She'd expected him to demand the reason for her sudden change of heart, but instead he said, 'It no longer matters,' and left, walking lithely down the path, tall and big and supremely confident.

Clammy with reaction, Sanchia forced the door closed and turned, stumbling along the passage like a sleepwalker. Uncaring, unseeing, she walked into her bedroom and across to the dressing table. 'Oh, Great-Aunt Kate,' she said hoarsely as she picked up the only photograph she had of her, 'I'm sorry.'

Late that afternoon she walked out of the house and down the path. Heat moistened the flyaway strands of her hair, clung to her temples, settled weightily over her. She couldn't bear to stay in the silent house alone with her thoughts; even worse was the prospect of her two flatmates' return.

She'd drive to one of Auckland's beaches and watch people enjoying themselves. Although it was a weekday the summer holidays meant that the beaches would be full of kids and parents. She needed, she decided, to sit mindlessly in a crowd and let the noise and the fun and the sheer humanity of it wash over her.

A horrified glance in the mirror had persuaded her to apply cosmetics to hide the shadows under her eyes; nailing her colours to the mast of pride, she'd chosen to wear tailored linen trousers the same smoky green as her eyes and a silky white singlet top that slid sensuously across her breasts. She might *feel* like something found on the beach after a spring tide, but there was no need to look like it.

The gate clicked behind her; she turned and began to walk along the hot, petrol-scented footpath towards her car, ignoring the rush-hour traffic.

She hadn't taken more than three steps when a car drew up beside her. Even before she recognised the driver, she knew who it was. She stopped and watched in frozen silence as the door opened and Caid got out.

For a moment she stared at him, almost convinced she'd summoned him by sheer force of will and longing, but her imagination hadn't produced the tall, compelling force of nature that was Caid Hunter.

'You're crying!' he said curtly, grasping her elbow.

A short toot brought both their heads up. 'Who's that?' Caid demanded.

'Rose—the woman who owns the house.' Sanchia waved in a distracted way as Rose drove into the gateway.

Before she was able to unscramble her mind enough to think a coherent thought he'd bundled her into the front seat of his car.

'I am *not* crying,' she snapped, but he slammed the door on her and strode around the front of the car.

Once behind the wheel, he pulled away from the pavement. 'You look as though you have been,' he grated.

She swallowed and demanded, 'What's going on?'

'We need to talk, but not now, not here. Leave it until we get home.'

He meant *his* home—or one of his homes; in this case, the top floor of a graciously refurbished apartment building on the harbour. Sanchia accompanied him into the private penthouse lift, waited in numb silence as it rose noiselessly, and stepped out with him into a lobby.

After a glittering glance at her Caid unlocked the door and stood back.

The decorator had clearly used Caid as inspiration for the colour scheme, choosing a quiet golden beige as the basic colour with dramatic touches of black, bronze and blue—pale ceramic tiles on the floor, pale walls, bronze and blue sofa, and two magnificent Eames chairs in black. Doorframes of polished wood warmed the room, as did plants selected for their sculptural qualities. Austere yet sensual, the apartment reflected his personality.

'What a stunning place,' Sanchia said, trying desperately to put a gloss of normality on the occasion.

'Thank you.' Eyes watchful in an inflexible face, he pulled his tie loose and dropped it over the back of the sofa. He'd already shed his jacket. The white shirt clinging to his broad shoulders was tucked into superbly cut trousers that measured narrow hips and long, muscular thighs in a purely male statement.

Sanchia's heart clamped into a knot of pain. Turning away, she stared through a window. 'You have a fantastic view.'

The westering sun laid a wash of rich amber over the scene. Beyond the wide deck stretched the harbour, a sleek, anchored warship on the far side denoting the naval base on the North Shore. A fat little ferry chugged towards the suburb of Devonport, rapidly overtaken by a large white catamaran on its way to one of the outer islands.

So peaceful, so Auckland—and so completely alien to the turmoil of apprehension that churned inside her. Acutely vulnerable, as though someone had taken to her emotions with a food mixer, Sanchia inhaled slowly and carefully before composing her features into a cool, questioning mask.

'What exactly do you want to talk to me about?' she asked in a stiff voice.

'First of all,' he said, watching her closely, 'how did it feel to confront Robert Atkins?'

'At first I was scared witless,' she said, carefully not looking at him, 'and then—he just looked sleazy and cheap and useless. A nothing of a man.'

Because for her now Caid was the standard she used to measure all other men.

'Are you still afraid of him?'

'No. I despise him, but—I'm not twelve any more. I find it hard to believe that I demonised him all those years.'

Caid nodded, his keen gaze fixed onto her face. 'You did it because he brutalised you when you were twelve and vulnerable.'

'Well, it's over now, thank God.' And thank Caid, she thought.

'Why did you say you'd sell the Bay to me?'

She looked away, her mind scurrying to find some reason she could give him without sounding like a lovesick idiot.

The corners of his chiselled mouth tilted into a humourless smile. 'Tell me the truth,' he invited softly. 'We've got the rest of a long summer day, and then there's the night.' An undercurrent of intimacy ran beneath the dispassionate words.

Rigid, her cheeks stung by spots of colour, she refused to lower her lashes. 'Because unless Cathy's changed a lot, she's spent all the money she stole from you.'

He surveyed her with half-closed eyes. 'So? You said once that you had no moral obligation to see me recompensed, and you were right.'

'I was wrong. Great-Aunt Kate would have made sure you got the money,' Sanchia said quietly.

His mouth tightened. 'She wasn't—and neither are you—responsible for Cathy's debts. So why the change of heart, Sanchia?'

She could have borne his shouting better than this purring mockery. Her frigid gaze clashed with his. 'Perhaps because I'm not greedy and self-serving and debauched.'

A muscle jumped in his jaw. 'I didn't mean it! You must have known I was stupidly, recklessly angry.' He laughed, a chilling, unamused sound. 'When we made love the second time I thought—that's it, at last you'd

learned to trust me! It was—well, it was a transcendental experience.'

Sanchia's heart jumped in her breast.
Surely—

He resumed in a voice that killed any chance
of hope, 'The very next day I found out that
you'd been planning all along to give the Bay
to the Council.'

Sanchia's brain had dissolved, collapsed.
She wanted—needed—to shake her head vio-
lently, in the hope it might marshal her
thoughts, but she couldn't move. So she drew
in a long silent breath. 'I knew you wouldn't
like it.' The words came out defiantly, aggres-
sive enough to be a challenge.

'You're too perceptive,' he retorted sarcas-
tically. He paused, reining in his anger so that
when he spoke again it was in a detached tone.
'You said once that your great-aunt wanted to
safeguard the pohutukawas and the butterfly
tree.'

'Yes.'

He gave her a keen glance. 'Was it important to her that the public have access to the
Bay?'

Sanchia frowned, trying hard to recall her aunt's words. 'I don't think so,' she said at last. 'She hated the way so much of the coastline is being developed, and she wanted to safeguard the trees and the bush. The only way to do that is to make it a reserve.'

'For two intelligent women,' he said sardonically, 'you've caused yourselves—and me—an immense amount of trouble. If public access is not the issue, the simplest way to make sure that the land won't ever be developed is to put it into a special trust—the Queen Elizabeth the Second Trust.'

'I've heard of that—but isn't it for farmers?'

'It's mostly farmers who use it to protect land of outstanding natural beauty, but it's available to anyone. The land remains in the farmer's estate, but no one can fell the bush or develop the land.' He paused, his intent gaze searching her face. 'If you sell the Bay to me, I'll replant it in coastal forest and deed it to the Trust.'

For a second she thought that deliverance had come, until she remembered. Hiding her intense disappointment, she said, 'I can't—I've told the Council that I'm going to give them the land.'

He said calmly, 'If I deal with the Council, will putting the Bay into the QEII Trust satisfy your obsessive need to pay back what you feel you owe your great-aunt?'

'I—yes.'

He pinned her with a searching, unsparing glance. 'But you're not happy about it.'

How could she explain this emptiness? If she thought that she was anything more to him than a transcendental experience in bed she might try, but he didn't love her.

Before she could speak he said forcefully, 'Sanchia, you don't—didn't—owe your great-aunt anything. In the years you lived with her you gave her an entirely unexpected joy in life,' he said, his voice as unrelenting as his angular features. 'She loved you and wanted you to be happy—she'd have been appalled if she'd known that her desire to safeguard the Bay was going to cause you such trouble.'

Sanchia fixed her stare on the busy little world outside the window.

He paused, then went on deliberately, 'And my attitude didn't help.'

On the harbour a small yacht went about, its sail flapping for a second, then filling. The little yacht pulled away steadily, heading for the islands of the Gulf. Afraid to think, Sanchia kept her gaze riveted to it.

Caid said, 'I won't lie to you—the last thing I want is for the Bay to be turned into a reserve. But that wasn't why I was so bloody-minded about it.'

'So why were you?' Her voice sounded flat, uninterested.

'A variety of reasons,' he said ambiguously. 'I admired your loyalty yet I resented it. It wasn't long before I realised that it was because carrying out your aunt's last wishes meant more to you than I did. I wanted you to give in, to tell me it didn't matter, that the only thing that you cared about was me. I wanted you to surrender everything.'

Moisture dampened Sanchia's temples and she forgot to breathe. 'Why?' she croaked, turning her head slightly so that she could see him.

That beautiful mouth eased into an ironic smile. 'Can't you guess? It was arrogant of me, I know, especially as you never gave any indication that I meant more to you than a convenient way to get rid of your virginity.'

Her cheeks stinging with colour, she returned, 'You must have known that I didn't see it as anything to get rid of.'

'I wondered, when I realised that I was the first man you'd been able to relate to after your experience with that swine.' He spoke neutrally, watching her with hooded eyes.

Sanchia discarded words as soon as she chose them, then decided to be as frank as he was. 'You were—remember when you carried me back from the butterfly tree after I wrenched my ankle? That's when I realised that a man's touch could be comforting and reassuring and—exciting.' Hope battled with caution when she said warily, 'I didn't make love with you to get rid of my virginity.'

'So why did you?'

Suddenly pride no longer mattered; she'd take whatever she could get from him. Tension rode her without mercy as she said, 'I wanted you.' She met his eyes and said with a hint of defiance, 'I'd do the same again.'

It was an open invitation. When he ignored it, continuing to regard her from beneath half-lowered eyelids, the heat and colour in her skin colour ebbed away into the clammy chill of rejection.

Frowning, he said, 'After I told you to go I realised I'd made the Bay a test. If you'd given up on the reserve idea, it would have meant I was more important to you than Kate's bequest. I wanted all your fierce loyalty for myself, yet I'd offered you nothing in return.'

Words tumbled in free-fall through her brain, disconnected, unspoken. Was he going to suggest they resume their short-lived affair? She wanted so much more from him now…

'I still want your loyalty,' he said, his voice low and raw and uncompromising. 'And although I can promise you my loyalty in return, loyalty is not what this is all about.'

Her heart missed two beats before she found the courage to say, 'Then what is it all about?'

Through lips that barely moved he said, 'I want everything you can give.'

A wave of love overcame her, fired her eyes to brilliance, trembled through her lips. 'That's a two-way thing. I want everything *you* can give too,' she said steadily, each word a vow.

Raggedly he said, 'Sanchia, I love you.'

It was as simple as that. She smiled as he came towards her and said, 'And I love you.'

A long time later he tucked her head under his chin and murmured, 'Not that I believe you.'

Frowning, she said, 'What don't you believe?'

'That you want everything from me,' he said judiciously. 'My bad temper?'

By then she would have forgiven him anything. 'I never saw you lose it until that last day at the Bay.'

He pulled a strand of hair across her white breast, surveyed it gravely, then bent to kiss it and the smooth skin beneath. 'I've worked damned hard to keep it under control,' he admitted, 'and I can promise you I won't subject you to it when we're married.'

His statement cut though her composure like a blade. She twisted to look up into his face, but iron arms held her against his naked chest, against the stirring strength of his loins.

'You do want to marry me, I hope?' he asked, no longer able to mask the taut undertone. 'I've lived in hell's lowest circle since you left, but I didn't contact you because I wanted to get the Bay out of the way. It had become a symbol, and like all symbols it was too emotive, too important to deal with directly.'

'What would you have done if I'd insisted on handing it over to the Council?'

He lifted her face and surveyed it, the cobalt eyes clear and unwavering. 'Accepted it.' Then his mouth curved in a slow, teasing smile. 'I planned to have a lot of pleasure trying to get you to change your mind, but when I found I couldn't bear the thought of you suffering because you hadn't fulfilled Kate's wishes, I realised that what I felt for you—this elemental, completely out of control need to see you happy—had to be love.'

Sanchia told him quietly, 'I won't suffer. She wanted the place to be cared for. You'll do that.'

Piercing, probing, his gaze held hers, demanding the truth. She met it frankly.

His chest lifted and fell in a huge sigh—of relief, she realised with astonishment, and finally let herself believe that this was real, this was happening. Caid Hunter loved her, wanted to marry her. Deep inside a tight lump of apprehension dissolved, vanishing into nothingness.

'Not,' he said on a grim note, 'that I was going to let you slide through my fingers again, although I had no idea how to break through the impasse. I toyed with the idea of kidnapping you and making you my love slave—'

'Fat hope,' she purred, kissing his throat. Her heart shivered as she felt his response, and his taste filled her mouth. She whispered, 'You didn't have to *make* me anything. I think I fell in love with you when I was sixteen and you carried me back to the bach and made me laugh.'

He stretched lazily. She could feel him smile, feel the vibration of his voice as he said, 'That was when I realised I was far too interested in someone far too young. I didn't give it a chance to grow, but when I saw you three years ago I wanted something that even then I understood, in some dim part of my brain, you weren't ready for. I thought it was sex, but I wanted more.'

'I think that's why I ran,' she said, resting her cheek against the fine tangle of hair across his chest. 'It wasn't just the sex that terrified me, it was the secret realisation that if I gave myself to you, if I took you, nothing would ever be the same again.' She hesitated, then added solemnly, '*I'd* never be the same again.'

'Yes,' he said, his voice so quiet she had to strain to hear it. 'Always, beneath the heat and the fire and the promise of an unbearable ecstasy, there was the threat of something deeper, more primal—a loss of autonomy, of control. I've never admitted it until now, but that's the real reason I didn't come after you three years ago. I wasn't ready to give up that selfish feeling of being master of my own life. I couldn't bring myself to surrender.'

Sanchia nodded. 'It's frightening.'

'But glorious,' he said on a half-laugh. 'When I saw you jump back as the car shocked you, I thought, *Damn it all to hell, here she is*. It was like a rearrangement of my mental processes—everything just slid away to make room for you and you moved in and took over. Oh, I didn't admit it straight away—'

'You certainly didn't! You were overbearing and critical and—'

He stopped her with a swift, hard kiss. 'I was completely winded! And then we made love.' He stopped and said quietly, 'That was—I can't describe it. I warned you that making love changed everything—I didn't realise that it would change me too.'

Unprompted, the words tumbled out. 'You've made love before.'

'And I won't lie and tell you that I haven't enjoyed it.' His hand came to rest on her thudding heart. 'But I'd never made love with someone I love.' His voice deepened, became rough. 'My heart, my darling girl, I can't tell you what it was like for me. Like being reborn. Like being handed paradise on a platter—all I ever wanted in one slim, silky body, one lovely smile, one pair of green, depthless eyes, one fierce, inconvenient loyalty. Then this whole bloody business about the Bay exploded in my face and I could see you weren't going to give an inch. What made it worse was that I could understand how you felt—and I admired and coveted your loyalty. Of course I didn't want a reserve next door, but that wasn't why I blew up.'

Sanchia's brows shot up.

'You'd hidden the truth from me,' he said calmly. 'I hated that, but not as much as I hated the prospect that you'd deliberately seduced me, possibly to keep me off-balance until you'd got the reserve through.'

She sat bolt upright and glowered down at the man she loved, magnificently naked in the huge bed, all flagrantly golden maleness. 'I wouldn't ever—'

'I know,' he said, his eyes appreciating her complementary nudeness, white and slender with her black hair in wild disarray.

He reached up and pulled her down, smoothing the mass of silk back from her indignant face. When she still fixed him with a simmering stare he kissed each green eye closed. 'It was only a momentary suspicion; you gave me so much, all of yourself, that I knew it couldn't be true. That's when I realised that I loved you. And, selfishly, I wanted you to love me enough to sell me the Bay. Today, when you told me I could have it, I realised that I'd been testing you, and I was ashamed.'

Caid kissed her forehead and stroked the hair back from it, his hand tender amongst the midnight strands, soothing and exciting her at the same time.

Sanchia muttered, 'But you ignored me!'

'I wanted to deal with Cathy first.'

'Oh.' Her aunt's name chilled her. 'What are you going to do with them?'

He lifted her chin and looked into her eyes. 'I'd like very much to kill him, but I'm not going to jeopardise our future so I settled for scaring the hell out of him. They've both signed documents admitting the fraud. While they keep out of our life and out of the news, they're safe enough.'

Sanchia considered this, then nodded. 'Thank you.' She shivered as he ran a lazily possessive hand from her throat to her hip.

'When you offered me the Bay it seemed like a peace offering, a very small, tentative olive branch. It was like seeing the sun after winter at the South Pole.'

'You said it no longer mattered. I thought it meant nothing.' She paused, then sighed and said, 'That I meant nothing.'

He lifted his head. 'You're all I ever want— all I'll want for the rest of my life.' Incredibly, his voice shook. 'When are we going to get married?'

She had to swallow an obstruction in her throat before she was able to say, 'Whenever you want.'

'In three days' time?' he pressed.

'Won't your mother want a big wedding?'

His chest moved beneath her cheek. 'Of course she will,' he said. 'But she's terrified I'll let you get away again. She's been giving me reproachful glares ever since you left.'

When Sanchia didn't answer he asked, 'What's the matter, my darling?'

She hesitated, then whispered, 'It just seems so—impossible. Everything. I'm terrified that I'll wake up and it will all have been a dream.'

His mouth very tender, he said, 'If it's a dream, we're both in it together, and it's going to last us a lifetime.'

A lean hand tilted her chin, lifting her face. Brilliant blue eyes scrutinised it, searching out the tender, blurred mouth, the skin made rosy by his lovemaking, then moved to her small, sensitive breasts.

'God,' he said thickly, his emotions finally breaking through the armour of his will. '*God*, you have no idea how much I love you. Tell me you'll be happy with me, Sanchia.'

She hugged him, kissed him, her hands slipping across his fine-grained skin with growing confidence. 'We'll be so happy together, my darling.' It was true; she had no doubts about it now. She murmured, 'I'll give the money you pay me for the Bay—after you've taken out the amount Cathy owes you—to charity. One dealing with conservation.'

Shock held him rigid for a second, then he relaxed and laughed. 'Kate would like that. You know, I'm actually looking forward to the problems that conscience of yours is going to cause me. Only, no more secrets, all right?'

'No more secrets,' she promised, secure at last in the safe haven of Caid's arms.

MILLS & BOON® PUBLISH EIGHT LARGE PRINT TITLES A MONTH. THESE ARE THE EIGHT TITLES FOR MARCH 2001

❧

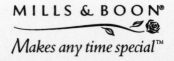

MILLS & BOON®

Makes any time special™

MILLS & BOON® PUBLISH EIGHT LARGE PRINT TITLES A MONTH. THESE ARE THE EIGHT TITLES FOR APRIL 2001

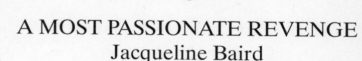

A MOST PASSIONATE REVENGE
Jacqueline Baird

HER SISTER'S BABY
Alison Fraser

THE CHRISTMAS CHILD
Diana Hamilton

BACK IN THE MARRIAGE BED
Penny Jordan

THE BABY GIFT
Day Leclaire

THE SPANISH HUSBAND
Michelle Reid

BRIDE BY DECEPTION
Kathryn Ross

WORTHY OF MARRIAGE
Anne Weale

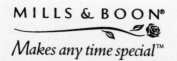

MILLS & BOON®

Makes any time special™